A Beautifully Broken CHRISTMAS

BRENDA S. ANDERSON

Paperback ISBN: 978-1-951664-12-1

The four short stories within the book originally appeared in The Mosaic Collection's Christmas Anthologies.

"A Christmas Homecoming" (previously published in "A Star Will Rise", 2020)
"A Beautiful Christ-mess" (previously published in "Hope is Born", 2019)
"Broken Noel" (previously published in "The Heart of Christmas", 2021)
"The Home for Christmas Challenge" (previously published in "A Thrill in the Air", 2023)

Cover Photo from Depositphotos

Second Edition published 2025

Vivant Press
Minneapolis, Minnesota

www.BrendaAndersonBooks.com

Printed in the United States of America

WELCOME

TO THE MOSAIC COLLECTION

We are sisters, a beautiful mosaic united by the love of God through the blood of Christ.

Several times a year, The Mosaic Collection releases faith-based novels and anthologies in a variety of genres. Our stories range from romance and suspense to literary and women's fiction.

Join our Mosaic reader family and discover soul-affirming stories of truth and hope.

mosaiccollectionbooks.com

Join our Reader Community, too!www.facebook.com/groups/TheMosaicCollection

A COMING HOME SERIES NOVELETTE

A CHRISTMAS Homecoming

BRENDA S. ANDERSON

A CHRISTMAS HOMECOMING

A Coming Home Series Novelette

"Our love story is definitely not typical. It began on a day not unlike this one, when your grandfather was on his way to propose to his girlfriend. Only two weeks later, he proposed to me."

Marlene Prestidge can't wait to leave the farm to study art in Paris. Now that her brother is coming home from the war in Vietnam, she finally has her chance. Until helping a stranded motorist leads to a chain of events that could forever put her dream on hold.

A *Coming Home Series* novelette

This story originally appeared in
The Mosaic Collection's 2020 Christmas anthology,
A Star Will Rise.

Dedication

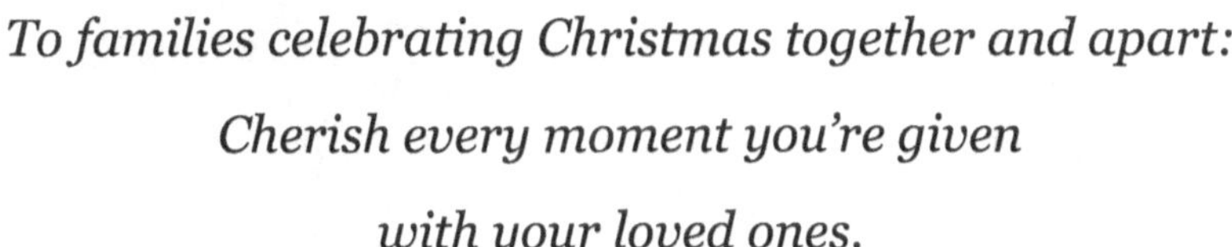

To families celebrating Christmas together and apart:
Cherish every moment you're given
with your loved ones.

Come, Thou Long Expected Jesus

This was going to be a Christmas to remember—Marlene Brooks felt it in her chilled bones as their pickup rumbled over snowy roads. She rubbed her gloved hands together while watching snow blow past the window of the truck—whooshing by too quickly. Over the fifty-plus years they'd known each other, her husband always had a leadfoot.

"Bernie, slow down." The words slid from her mouth. She could never resist passenger-seat driving. The last thing they needed today was to land in the ditch when the entire family was going to be home for the first time in years! She didn't have a second to waste.

He just laughed and gave her leg a pat, his way of reassuring her. "The last time I ended up in a ditch was fifty-one years ago, and it changed my life." He shot her a quick glance and his crooked smile still set loose hummingbirds in her stomach. Oh, the man could charm her.

"Well, I would prefer no life-changing events happen today, please." Just a happy, family celebration of their golden anniversary, two weeks late to combine with Christmas and Thanksgiving. Their home would be filled with boisterous laughter and off-key carol singing, lingering hugs and comfort food shared between their children, the spouses, grandchildren, and several unofficially-adopted grandchildren. Twenty-two people would be gathering, worshiping the Savior, in their home on Christmas Day—tomorrow!—and she couldn't wait to see them all.

Their life overflowed with blessings.

Bernie yawned. "I might need a nap before family arrives. I think the pastor this morning nearly put me to sleep."

Her eyes snapped open. "A nap? When I've got a to-do list long enough for three people to handle?"

"I know, darling, but." He rotated his jaw. "Must not have slept well last night. I'm feeling a bit lightheaded." He cleared his throat. "You don't happen to have some heartburn pills in that purse of yours, do you?"

She sighed and dug out an antacid tablet. The man had farmed for forty years, up before the roosters each one of those days, getting in a daily workout that would be the envy of Arnold Schwarzenegger, and yet when it came to helping in the house . . .

Goodness, who was she to complain? She closed her eyes and lifted thanks to their Creator for His abundance. Their fifty years together hadn't been problem-free, but every obstacle had strengthened their spiritual muscles.

So, yes, this anniversary was one worth celebrating.

"Marlene . . ." Bernie's normally-strong voice came out weak, breathy.

Her eyes whipped wide open, and she jerked toward her husband.

Only one hand gripped the steering wheel, the other massaged his left shoulder. "I'm not feeling—"

The pickup veered onto the side of the road. Snow gripped the tires, pulling the truck into the ditch. It careened toward an unfrozen pond.

"Bernie! Stop!" The horn began blaring.

She glanced at her husband, now slumped over the steering wheel. "Bernie!" She grabbed the wheel, pushed him back, and gasped. His eyes were closed, his body a dead weight, and his foot continued pressing on the accelerator.

They weren't slowing.

"Dear Jesus, help," she breathed out as she reached across the center console, attempting to knock his leg enough to disengage his foot from the accelerator. Failing, she gripped the gear shift and yanked it into neutral.

Deep snow tugged at the tires, finally bringing the truck to a stop at the pond's edge.

"Dear Jesus, Bernie has to be okay." She removed a glove and touched his cheeks. Cold. She felt for a pulse in his neck. Nothing. Pressed harder. "Bernie, don't you go dying on me now. We've got a houseful of people coming to see you."

There. A faint tick in his neck. Praise God!

"Good. You're listening to me for once. I know you don't like ambulances, but you'll have to swallow your pride." Her heart hammering, she dug through her purse, searching for her phone, and a rare curse word entered her thoughts as she recalled leaving her cell on the kitchen counter.

"Bernie, you have your phone?" He had to have it. He never went anyplace without it. "I'm not getting fresh, dear, just need to call 911." She dug her hand between his back and the truck seat, praying he'd put it in his right pocket, yet knowing it wouldn't be there. A creature of habit, he always carried his phone in his left pocket.

Getting into it from here would be impossible. That meant she had to get out of the truck and walk around.

She squeezed her door handle and pushed. No movement. The truck leaned right, and snow crowded halfway up the door. She attempted rolling down the window, but it was frozen shut. That left the driver's side back door. Which meant she'd have to climb over the console to the backseat.

Once upon a time, that wouldn't have been an issue, but at seventy-three years of age, her body didn't bend that way.

She could do it. She *would* do it. Quickly.

"Bernie, you behave yourself. No wise comments." Talking to him helped, didn't it?

She turned, pulled her right leg up on the seat, followed by the left, then squeezed between the front seats, and crawled onto the back bench. Victory. She reached for the door, squeezed the handle. No movement.

Oh, it was locked.

From the front with child safety locks. God, can't one thing be easy?

"Okay, honey, just reaching over your shoulder for the door lock." She got a whiff of his aftershave and that nearly summoned tears, but she couldn't cry now. He needed her strong. She hit the unlock button and heard a click. "Thank You, Jesus."

She tried the door again. This time, it opened.

"I'll be right there, sweetheart. Just hold on." She got out of the truck, shuffled through the snow, around the open door, and tugged open the driver's side door, Bernie slumped against it. "Oh, no you don't." She pushed him back up, thankful for all the years of bale throwing that had made her strong.

"You better have your phone in your back pocket, mister." She squeezed her hand between the seat and his back and felt the phone. Yes! Now to pull it out.

Her fingers were numb from the freezing air and refused to grip the phone. She withdrew her hand, blew on her stiff fingers to warm them, and tried again. Reaching below his backside, she yanked on the phone. It didn't budge. Goodness, the man weighed a ton.

"Bernie, dear, when we get home, you are going on a diet." Holding her breath and sending up silent prayers, she tried again. It loosened.

She gripped it tighter. Pulled. It moved. Tug. Movement. Grunt. Pull. It yanked free, thank the Lord. She awoke the phone, typed in his security code. Wrong. Typed it in again. It unlocked. She dialed 9-1-2. Grrr. Delete. Typed 1. Listened.

"9-1-1. What's your emergency?"

Marlene's chin quivered. "It's my husband. I think he had a heart attack."

Still, Still, Still

"Grandma?"

Marlene forced her eyes open and looked to the left. Nathan and Tessa, his girlfriend of the past year, approached.

He sat beside her in the hospital's family waiting room and put an arm around her back. "How are you? How's Grandpa?"

"I . . . I don't know." She checked her watch. It had been one hour since they'd arrived at the hospital. She looked down the hallway the doctor had used after informing Marlene that Bernie had suffered a myocardial infarction—a fancy term for heart attack—that he required immediate coronary bypass surgery to unclog calcified arteries, and that the procedure could take hours.

"Well, we're here for you now." He pressed a kiss to her cheek. "Mom and Dad and the sibs are on their way. Uncle Ricky and family arrived at the airport. With the weather, it'll be a while before they get here. Lauren and Jet left

Minneapolis an hour ago with Doran and Meghan. They left Ellie with friends."

Marlene closed her eyes and shook her head. Cuddling that dear toddler of Doran and Meghan's would have lifted her spirits, but who was she to complain. The rest of the family would be here, but this was not how she planned to celebrate. It was not the Christmas homecoming she'd hoped for. Bernie better pull through this, or she'd give him a good talking to.

"And Grandma?"

She pried open her eyes and looked up at her tall grandson who was too handsome for his own good. Thankfully, he had Tessa to keep him grounded. Words failed her, so she simply nodded for him to keep going.

"We have some good news for you."

She sat up straight, but a smile wouldn't come. "Good news is exactly what I need."

"I thought so." Nate gripped his girlfriend's hand. "Tessa and I wanted you and Grandpa to be the first to hear." He raised her hand and displayed a ring. A teal stone with white gold. Unique and beautiful, just like Tessa. "We're engaged." He grinned. "Asked Tessa on Christmas Eve. Just like Grandpa asked you."

The happy news summoned tears she'd reined in. "Congratulations." Remaining seated, she opened her arms for the happy couple. As she hugged the two, she prayed their happiness wouldn't be scarred by today's events.

"Your parents don't know yet?"

Nathan grinned. "Nope. Wanted to tell you first. And we'll tell Grandpa as soon as he's out of surgery."

If he survives surgery . . .

No, she couldn't go there. He had to survive. Just because his father died from a heart attack, as did his brother, did not mean Bernie would too. He had way too much to live for.

"Your grandfather will be very happy for you. Tessa, dear, we're very blessed to have you as part of the Brooks family."

Tessa showed that pink-faced smile of a young girl in love while gripping Nathan's hand. "I couldn't have found a better family to join. You've all made me feel welcome."

That had been the goal, to always have the open chair, to make outsiders feel like part of the family.

"Nate told me you and Grandpa Bernie have a unique story. Would you mind telling me?"

What a wise child, helping to separate Marlene from her grief, even if only for a moment.

Marlene sat up and patted the chair beside her. Nathan sat on one side and Tessa on the other, bookending her with love.

"Our love story is definitely not typical. It began on a day not unlike this one, when Nathan's grandfather was on his way to propose to his girlfriend. Only two weeks later, he proposed to me."

Fifty-One Years Earlier

It was supposed to be the best Christmas season ever, but when you're only twenty-two, there aren't many Christmas days to compare to. Still, as I drove toward home two weeks before Christmas, anticipation filled me.

My big brother was coming home from Vietnam! The war. I still shiver thinking of not only the horrors my brother had seen and suffered, but also how despicably the troops were greeted upon returning home. They were going from one war to another, just a different type of battlefield. But my brother would be heralded by our family for his thirteen months of service with the Marines. The bag beside me in the pickup, filled with American flags, was proof.

He was already back on U.S. soil—he'd called Momma and Pops earlier that day saying everything was on schedule and he'd be home at about seven PM, a mere hour away. I couldn't wait to see him.

And then I could finally leave the United States.

Paris, France, and its thousand-plus art museums called to me. With Byron home, he'd take over farm duties and I could leave home guilt free.

The tires skidded, drawing my attention back to the road. It wouldn't do any of us any good if I landed in the ditch. Some *welcome home* that would be for Byron: his first job would be to rescue his helpless little sister from the ditch. He'd never let me live that down.

Slowing, I flicked the wipers on the pickup, pushing

snowflakes off to the side. A vortex of flakes streamed toward me, harder now than even half a second before. The roads would be slick before long.

Lights reflecting off my rearview mirror blinded me as a vehicle too quickly narrowed the gap between us. Whoever approached was nuts.

He veered into the other lane as my truck climbed the hill. Another vehicle crested that hill from the opposite direction, but that didn't slow the passing car. Instead, he zoomed faster, and I slowed. Just in time, the sports car swung in front of me, barely missing my front bumper. Made me want to hurl some bad words his way, but the taste of soap lingered from my testing-teenager years.

The approaching car whizzed past, blowing up a cloud of snow, and the crazy driver in front fishtailed. I slowed more, creating distance between my pickup and the fool.

The car swerved again, spun a full donut, right into the ditch, facing the wrong way.

I couldn't help but laugh as I puttered past. Served him right. The nearest home was mine, and that was two miles away. That would be an awful chilly walk if they couldn't get back on the road.

Which means you should stop and help.

Words from Momma and Pops invaded my brain. But Bryon was coming home. I didn't have time.

You always have time to help.

Dratted conscience.

I slowed to a stop, shifted to reverse, backed up past the red El Torino, and pulled off the side of the road. They weren't in deep, but the driver's efforts at jiggling the sports car back and forth were just digging them deeper. A board—which I had plenty of in the truck bed—and some elbow grease should free them.

I put on my gloves and cap, zipped my jacket, and stepped out of the pickup.

And glanced at the driver and his passenger.

Two familiar faces.

Yippee . . .

Didn't matter. I was going to offer a hand because it was the right thing to do, and no one would say Marlene Prestidge refused to help a stranded motorist.

The driver, Bernie Brooks, shook his head as I approached. If he wanted to stay in the ditch, I could accommodate.

Still, I rapped on his window, and he rolled it down.

"I'll give you a push," I offered.

Beside him, Elaine snickered. "You?"

Bernie pinned his girlfriend—or was it *wife* now?—with a look I wouldn't want to be on the receiving end of. Then he actually gave me a sheepish glance. "I'd be glad for help, Darlene."

Really? "It's *M*arlene." I emphasized the M. After going to the same school all our lives, and the same church, you'd think he'd get my name right. Guess those football star stereotypes weren't too far off. He had been dating the head cheerleader since their mid-teens. Why would he notice the artist nerd?

"Sorry about that." He began opening his door.

"No, stay put. I've got a piece of plywood in the truck. That and a little push should get you out."

He continued to open the door and motioned to Elaine to move over. "Two is better than one. We'll get out faster."

True.

Only then did I notice they were dressed to the nines. Bernie in a three-piece, powder-blue polyester suit, Elaine in a sparkly maxi-dress. He'd totally mess himself up by helping.

"It's obvious you two have a special evening planned. Get back in. I'll push."

"Our special evening will happen much faster if I help."

Stubborn jerk. "If I were a guy, you'd say go ahead."

He snorted at that, of all things. "My two sisters would crucify me if I were a male chauvinist." He got out and slammed the door. "I'm helping because it's the right thing to do."

"Oh." Our parents must have been on same wavelength when raising kids. "Fine. And I'm sorry." I'm really not a women's lib snob, but the current culture pinned it in the forefront of my mind.

"No problem." Bernie walked with me to the back of my pickup, his dress shoes and pant legs becoming frosted with snow. Together we lifted the snow-coated piece of plywood from the truck bed then laid it on the ground in front of his car and pressed it beneath the front tires as much as we could. Then he walked to the driver's side door and motioned to Elaine. "We'll push. You drive."

"Fine," she snapped at him, and he winced.

"Trouble in paradise?" I asked as we trudged through snow to the back of his car. It sure was a fine ride.

He laughed. "You could say that." We reached the back of the car and braced our gloved hands on the trunk. "Reservations at Billy's Supper Club were for twenty minutes ago."

"Uh-oh."

"Exactly." He showed Elaine two thumbs-up. Hopefully, she'd take the hint. "I was going to propose."

Going to?

The car started up, and Elaine put it into gear. The tires spit snow and dirt back at us as we pushed.

The front tires finally gained traction on the plywood, and the vehicle shot forward, missing the back of my truck by a hand's width.

Tonight was a full evening of near misses it seemed. We walked to my truck as Elaine pulled the car around.

"You're still going to propose, right?"

He laughed. Seemed to be his go-to reaction for discomfort. "After tonight, I don't know if she'll want me." He stuck his hands deep into the pockets of his polyester pants.

"If she loves you, it'll all work out."

"Yeah, I suppose." The car pulled up beside us, and Bernie held up a finger to Elaine, asking her to wait. "I'll walk you to your door."

"It's not necessary."

"Maybe, but it is the right thing to do."

Huh. What was with this guy?

"So, what brings you out on a night like this?"

And now small talk from a guy who'd never noticed me before, a guy who called me *D*arlene.

"My brother's coming back from 'Nam tonight." Actually, he was probably home already. Well, I'd have a story to tell the family.

"Vietnam, huh?" He opened my pickup door and motioned for me to climb up. "Thank him for his service. It's been a rough road for the troops."

"I'll give him the message. Thank you." I gripped the door handle. "You've got a bit of a tough road ahead, too."

He scratched his nearly black hair. "Tell me about it. Thanks again for your help."

"Glad to do it." I closed my door and watched him jog back to his car. From the second he opened the door, Elaine's mouth was flapping, and I doubted she was telling Bernie what an awesome guy he was.

All I knew was that she didn't deserve him.

But that was none of my business. Besides, I was due at home about fifteen minutes ago. The family would all wonder what had distracted me this time. This time, I had a reason they'd all appreciate.

The drive home took me another five minutes. Not wanting to end up in the ditch myself, I slowed my pace, though my excitement at seeing my big brother for the first time in over a year pushed me to hurry.

A pickup I hadn't seen before sat in our driveway. Byron? Excitement bubbled inside me as I ran to the house, right past Rex, our German shepherd, who gave a sad yelp. I leaped up the concrete steps and into the house. From the mud room, I scanned the kitchen. Dirty plates and cups sat in the sink, but no sign of life, which meant they were likely congregating in the front room.

Disregarding Momma's voice speaking to my conscience, I kicked off my boots and left them dripping where they landed. For this, Momma would forgive me.

I hurried through the kitchen and dining room and into the front room. He sat on the davenport with Pops and Momma, speaking in deep tones I couldn't decipher. Tears nearly welled up at the sight of him. Jeepers, I knew I'd missed my big brother, but tears?

He glanced my way and stood as I entered the room. Had he grown taller? Or was it just the maturity I read in his face, his broad shoulders, his perfectly-upright stance?

"You going to stand there gaping at me, or are you gonna give me a hug?" That familiar smirk added the boyishness back to his features.

"I don't know." I couldn't resist giving back. "I'm thinking you deserve a knuckle sandwich for staying away so long. About time you get home and help with the chores."

"About that . . ." He scratched his head and looked at Momma and Pops as if seeking their permission to speak. He was a soldier, had fought in the war. Didn't that alone give him permission? He nodded to the recliner near him. "Have a seat."

Translation: I have something bad to tell you that you're not going to like.

So, I balked at first, but not listening wouldn't delay whatever he needed to tell me, it would just put off adjusting to whatever bad news he had.

"Are you all right?" I finally sat on the edge of the recliner and studied his face and hands. Had he contracted some disease over there? Swallowed some cancer-causing poison?

"Yeah. I'm good." He folded his hands in his lap and looked at me directly with haunted eyes that had likely seen too much death.

"But . . .?"

He inhaled and blew it out slowly. A procrastinating tactic I was too familiar with.

"But I'm not coming home. I re-enlisted. I'm going back after Christmas."

"You what?" My legs gained a will of their own and propelled me from the chair. "That's bogus." How dare he re-enlist? He was supposed to come home and stay. Help Pops with the farm so I could go to Paris and study. Pops and Momma couldn't handle the farm alone. They'd said so more than once.

Tears threatened again, but this time they were feel-sorry-for-myself tears. Crossing my arms over my chest, I turned toward the window featuring a snowstorm that raged harder now as if it too were angry at Byron's announcement.

"I don't understand." I forced out the words, trying to maintain an even keel.

"It's where I belong." His deep voice sounded behind

me close enough to feel his warm breath on my neck. “Serving my country. It’s the right thing to do.”

Oh, I was beginning to hate that phrase. I refused to sniffle and give away the fact that I was miffed at him. “And what about my plans? What about the farm?”

“Your mother and I . . .” Now Pops stood too close, crowding me. “It’s time we considered selling.”

And give up their dream because their kids were selfish? I hugged myself tighter. Weren’t there other options? “What about hiring someone? Other farmers do it all the time.”

“And they have problems all the time with their hired hands.” Pops shook his head. “Not worth the hassle.”

A deep sigh escaped my throat. Sure, I was being dramatic, but I didn’t want to be the reason Pops stopped farming. He loved it all. Working with the cows. Growing crops. He was meant to be a farmer, and doing some other job would slowly kill him.

“Then maybe you sell a few cows, some land. Still farm, but on a smaller scale.”

“Marly, dear.”

Ah, Momma. Always the pacifier.

“Your father and I have given this a lot of thought.”

So, they hadn’t just learned about Byron’s plans tonight? I whipped toward my big brother, who I really wanted to wallop right then. “They knew before tonight?”

He just shrugged, the jerk.

“And surprise me with this groovy Christmas present. Gee thanks.” As if it were all about me. But at that moment, that was what my selfish feelings were communicating. My best option was to remove myself from that room before I said anything else stupid.

"I'm sorry." I took a breath and turned to face my family. "I know I'm being selfish. I just need time to absorb this, okay?" Which meant going to the basement to slap paint on a canvas.

Jaw clenched, I slammed a clean canvas on my easel and asked myself: Did God require that I give up my dream so Dad could live his?

Breath of Heaven

"How's Dad doing?"

The worried interruption by her second son tore Marlene from the unsure past into the painful present. She looked up at Marcus. Janet, his wife, clung to his hand, and their two youngest children hurried to give Marlene hugs. Nothing was more healing than hugs from grandchildren.

She kissed a tear from Jaclyn's cheek. "Say a prayer for your grandpa."

"We have been." From a young age, Joshua had been a spiritual leader and Grandpa's woodworking buddy. Though he was trying to be brave, the fear shown in his eyes.

"Sit by me." She gestured to Marcus, Nathan, and Joshua to bring chairs into a circle and they all sat.

"How's Dad?" Marcus's normally sure voice wobbled, only enough for a mother to detect. He had the looks and temperament of his father. And the heart. Oh, Marcus had a big heart that easily bled.

"We have not heard." Not since they'd wheeled him away from her, down a hallway, and through doors that led to who knew where? Would she see him again this side of heaven?

If not, she would rejoice for him even as her heart broke.

"I'll go talk to someone." Her son headed toward the nurses' desk, but she called him back.

"Let them be. It's a busy night. Lots of accidents."

"But—"

"But sit yourself down. I'm telling Tessa Bernie's proposal story."

Catching her hint, his intensity cooled, and he joined the circle. "One of my favorite stories."

"Mine too. Now, where was I?"

The day after hearing Byron's news, I couldn't stay home. My anger still simmered against him. Or maybe it wasn't anger as much as self-pity. How could I be angry with someone wanting to serve our country? During wartime?

What if he didn't come back?

Pops needed his farm, especially now.

But until Byron reported for duty, he could do chores, so I could escape.

Our small town didn't have a lot of places to go for entertainment, not like nowadays. If you didn't feel like doing outdoor sports, then the biggest hangout was the indoor mall, so that was where I headed even though I'd already finished Christmas shopping. There I would be surrounded by harried shoppers. Most would ignore me, just the way I liked it.

I purchased a couple new paints before grabbing a bite from a fast-food joint. I then spotted a bench that wasn't already occupied by bored husbands and hurried to it. Beside me, I felt someone else rushing in the same direction, so I sped up and beat them. Ha!

"Marlene?"

Bernie?

I looked up at the person I'd raced and gestured for him to sit. "Sorry about that."

"You realize, if I really tried, I'd have beat you." With a food bag clutched in his hand, he smiled as he sat, but his eyes told a different story.

Should I ask about it? Nah. Wasn't any of my business.

"Thanks again for last night." He removed a wrapped burger from the bag. "It didn't end the way I'd planned, but I know now it was for the best."

Oh, no. "I'm sorry."

He shrugged. "Turns out while we were away at college, she found someone else. The thing is, when she told me, I almost felt relief."

"It still hurts, I'm sure."

"Well, other news I got last night hurts more." He clutched his burger but didn't bite.

I just stared at my sandwich. Why was he being so

chatty? Before last night, he'd spoken maybe two sentences to me other than what had been necessary for class assignments. Still, I felt compelled to listen. Maybe then he'd listen to my story. It would feel good to get my troubles off my chest.

"What happened?"

He stared down the mall corridor toward a line of children and mothers waiting to see Santa. "My brother's buying the farm."

Okay? I didn't have any backstory to gauge my response on. "And that's a bad thing?"

"Depends upon who you talk to. Dad's thrilled. He had a tractor accident a few years back and has been wanting to do something else. My brother and I picked up the slack so he wouldn't have to work so hard. With Harry taking over, I'd be his employee, and, to be honest, we don't get along that well. Already, he's bossing me around. I'd look for other work, but farming is all I've ever wanted to do. What I went to college for. It's in my blood."

Just like my father . . .

I sat up straight. This could be my opportunity! Pops knew the Brooks family. He'd know Bernie wasn't a slacker, right?

"How about working for my father?" Maybe I shouldn't have asked without permission, but this was an answer to my family's dilemma. Everyone could live their dreams.

"Your dad?"

"Byron's re-upping. My folks"— and I—"were counting on him for help."

A glimmer appeared in Bernie's too-attractive eyes. "You think he'd hire me?"

"There's one way to find out. Pops is home. Let's go ask."

"That'd be cool! I'm ready."

"You know where I live?"

He just cocked his head to the side.

Okay. Stupid question. Every farmer in the area knew each other and supported each other. That was how things were done back then.

"I'll meet you at my place."

"Be right behind you."

I think I prayed all the way home. If Pops hired Bernie, he could keep farming, Byron wouldn't have to feel guilty about leaving, I could study abroad, and Bernie wouldn't have to work for his brother. Each of us would be winners. How could Pops say, "No"?

About fifteen minutes later, I was seated beside Bernie at our kitchen table. No surprise, Momma served pie she'd just removed from the oven. She always seemed to know when someone was going to drop in. In farm country, that happened daily. Sometimes several times a day. Momma was always prepared, and Pops loved sharing a coffee with his farm colleagues.

I remained a quiet observer as Pops, Byron, and Bernie swapped livestock stories, crop plans, and the low price of milk. Though Bernie was my age, Pops treated him as an equal. Bernie also raved over Momma's pie, adding more brownie points. No way would Pops turn down our offer.

"What brings you here, Bernard?" So, Pops knew this wasn't a casual visit.

"Well, sir, I'm looking for a job as a hired hand."

Pops said nothing, just raised his brows.

"My brother's buying our farm, and we both know I wouldn't be long for the place with him in charge."

"Hmmm." Pops sat back in his chair and crossed his arms. "If I hire you, what happens when you and I disagree? What's to stop you from finding something new?"

"I . . . well . . ." Bernie slouched, scratching the side of his cheek.

Uh-oh, there went our plans.

But then Bernie sat up, tall and straight. "When I make a commitment, sir, I keep it."

"Son." Pops crossed his hands on the table and shook his head. "I believe you, but I'm also very aware of human nature. I've found that those who work the farm the best are those who have a stake in the business."

"If you're talking investing in the farm, I don't have cash now—just spent it on college. Got an agricultural studies degree—"

"Son, I appreciate that. I do. I know you're a hard worker. Your father's said as much. If I had more time to consider, I might give you a try, but there's an offer on the table for the farm—"

"What?" More secrets kept from me? I threw down my fork and it clattered onto the floor. I left it there. "When did this happen?"

"It's been in the works for months, and the man wants an answer by Christmas." Pops looked me in the eye, and I saw sorrow in his. "I can't turn down this opportunity on the chance that Bernard will keep his commitment."

"But I will be here. Farming is your life."

"And art is yours." He shook his head. "It's time you pursued your dream."

"But—"

"Marlene, dear." Momma, talking in that placating tone again. Made Marlene angrier yet. "Your father and I are at peace with this decision."

"Well I'm not." Though I was twenty-two, I threw a tantrum worthy of someone twenty years younger and stomped out of the house. No jacket. No mittens. Just boots and a whole bunch of attitude. I hurried to the barn and climbed up in the loft, where cats would soon fill my lap.

I wasn't disappointed. There was something about a cat's purr that removed tension from stress. But they didn't warm me enough. I could have at least grabbed my coat on the way out of the house. Idiot.

"You okay?"

Apparently, the cats and I weren't alone.

Bernie walked toward me, carrying my winter jacket. "Your mom said to bring this to you."

I gratefully accepted the coat. "Sorry you had to witness that. I'm usually more grown up, but I'm not dealing well with all these changes."

He gestured toward the bale beside mine. "Do you mind?"

"Fine with me."

He sat, and a cat found a home on his lap. "Can I ask you a question?"

"You just did."

"Ha ha." He stroked the tortoiseshell's fur. "You know my dream. What's yours?"

"Huh?"

"Back in the house, your dad alluded to you being able to pursue your dream. I'm just curious."

No one had ever asked that before. A couple of friends knew, but not acquaintances, not people who would mock me for being foolish.

"You'll think it's stupid."

He grinned, and it was a very nice grin, which made me angry that I'd noticed. "No dream is stupid."

I stared across the hayloft at the piles of bales strewn together. Remove one and you could have an avalanche. Just like Pops selling the farm could result in an avalanche of lost dreams.

My hands wrung together as I forced the words out. "I've always wanted to study art in Paris." I stopped, waited for the ridicule.

"Far out!" The slang sounded foreign coming from his mouth.

"Yeah, that's what everyone says, but most think it's because the idea is far out in the field. They think it's a crazy idea."

"And you care what others think?"

I shrugged. "Sometimes, but that wouldn't stop me."

"So, now's your chance to go. I don't see what the problem is with your dad selling the farm."

"The problem is, farming is his passion, and it breaks my heart to think of him throwing it away when he has an amazing offer from you. We have to convince him that you're the answer."

"We? I don't think he'll listen to me."

"Okay. Me. I have to convince him. If I do, you get to farm, and I go to Paris. We all get what we want."

But as Momma often reminded me, what we want isn't always what God wants for us. Or maybe God desired that I pay more attention to Him.

It was then I decided I needed to up my prayer game and ask God for a solution.

O, Come All Ye Faithful

"Mom." A hand rested on Marlene's shoulder, one that always put her at ease. Deborah had that gift, which was why she'd gone into counseling.

Marlene looked up and back into the wise eyes of her daughter. Her middle child circled her arms around her neck in a hug that spoke love.

Debbie's youngest daughter pressed a chubby hand to Marlene's cheek. "I pway for Gwampa."

"Darling girl." I drew the precious child onto my lap. Lilly might be small for her age, and slow, as the world would define it, but no one had a bigger heart. "Your prayers are heard and felt."

"I know." Lilly beamed and leaned into me, nestling her head beneath my chin.

"Any word?" Debbie and Jerry joined the circle of adults. Their other two children sat with their cousins.

Marlene shook her head. "It's a tough surgery." And

Bernie wasn't young anymore. Had she been selfish giving permission to operate? What if Bernie survived, but not enough so he could truly live?

"As Lilly said, we're all praying." Debbie looked to her brother and his wife for confirmation, and they nodded. As did Nathan and his fiancée. Oh, how wonderful it was to say—or think—the word, fiancée. Nathan better tell the family soon or she was going to accidentally blurt it out.

"There's nothing more powerful than prayer." Marlene looked to Tessa. Needing to get her mind on something else, she'd gladly finish her story. "That's all I did in those two weeks leading up to Christmas Eve. Bernie and I. Every evening we'd meet at our church to pray, pleading for a solution to our problems and asking for peace with however God chose to answer. God certainly answered our prayers, but not at all in a way we'd anticipated."

And that was what frightened Marlene now. She wanted God to answer prayers with the answer she wanted, not the one He was likely to give.

I had never prayed so much in my life. The funny thing was, the more I prayed, the more time I spent with God, the more at peace I was with the situation. Now, don't get me wrong, I still wanted Pops to keep the farm and Bernie to work there. I still desperately wanted to go to Paris, but both Bernie and I had come to the point of saying, "Thy will be done," at the end of our prayers.

I don't think there's a more enlightening yet frightening prayer.

Something else was happening with me, too. Something completely unexpected and equally terrifying: I was beginning to like Bernie. He wasn't the arrogant athlete I'd pegged him as in high school. He was kind, thoughtful, selfless. And, oh yeah, he was a complete fox. Dark hair. Indigo eyes. Strong build. Oh my, I'd developed a crush.

The trick was, not letting him see that attraction when we got together for prayer before that evening's Christmas Eve service. After Christmas, unless God intervened, Pops would sell the farm, Byron would go wherever the military told him to go, and me? Well, I guessed I'd go to Paris. I should have been thrilled, but knowing Pops planned to work at the local implement dealer stole my joy, even on Christmas Eve.

Hopefully, prayer would restore that joy.

I arrived before Bernie at our usual prayer spot, the church library, and joy did start to seep in. Someone had dressed the room in bows and greenery. A wood-carved manger scene I'd never seen before occupied a shelf. It was exquisite. I picked up an angel and ran my finger over the feathered wings. The artist really had an eye for detail.

"Like it?"

Startled, I turned to Bernie, who'd somehow snuck up behind me.

"I love it." I returned the angel to the shelf. "Whoever carved it is talented."

"Thank you."

"Huh?"

He grinned, and my stomach did a traitorous somersault.

"You mean, you carved this?"

"Guess I did." He shrugged. "It's a hobby. I've always loved working with wood."

"You should sell your work."

"Nah. Then it becomes a job." He gestured toward the library door. "Changing the subject, would you mind praying outside tonight? The weather's perfect—for December that is—and I . . . I just feel closer to God when I'm outside. I can hear Him better."

One more thing to like about Bernie Brooks. Gah!

After putting on my coat and gloves, I followed him out the back of the church. Peace enveloped me as I stared up at the sky lit with thousands of stars.

"Beautiful, isn't it?"

"It is." I looked at him, only to find him staring at me. Even with my warm coat on, his piercing gaze gave me the goosebumps. I needed a quick diversion. "Let's sit." I pointed to a wood bench nestled in a garden area. During summer, the garden was beautiful.

He sat beside me. "Time to pray?"

I nodded, and he grasped my hand.

"I hope you don't mind."

Mind? My heart shot into my throat with the feel of his gentle strength. If he only knew what he was doing to me.

"Dear Lord," Bernie began the prayer. "It's us, back

again. After ignoring You for so long, it's a wonder You're not sick of us now, but You've invited us to Your throne, given us direct access, and that . . . it humbles me, Lord, to think You want to hear from us, and that You want to spend time with us. Listening. Advising."

"Amen," I added, not to close the prayer but to share my agreement with his words.

"You've been teaching me to listen to You, even when what You're saying makes no sense. Give me courage tonight to be obedient to You."

At that, I said nothing. Bernie's words scared me. He needed courage to do what?

Silence took over, and I had no words to fill the void. My hand remaining locked with Bernie's, I looked up at the stars. Watched them. Listened.

One seemed to beam brighter than the others. Could it be Mars? Venus maybe? I was clueless when it came to astronomy, I just knew I liked watching the night sky. Maybe that was the star the wise men followed to find Jesus.

Voices sounded on the other side of the church building, worshippers coming for the candlelight service. Our prayer time was coming to an end, and we hadn't asked for a solution to our problem, as we did every other night. We hadn't asked for peace with whatever answer God returned.

Maybe simply waiting and trusting was His answer.

"I have a question for you, Marlene."

That was a strange thing to say. Why not just ask the

question? "Okay?"

He cleared his throat, and his grip on my hand grew stronger. "Do you like me?"

Never have I been so grateful for the dark of night, but my cheeks' glow probably provided enough light to see the details of my face.

So, I just nodded.

"I mean, do you, uh, do you really like me?"

He had to have heard my heart leap at his voice. Get a grip, woman! Finally, I whispered out, "I do."

"Whew."

Beside me, I felt his whole body loosen and shift toward me, our knees touching.

"These last two weeks have been . . . strange. A good strange."

I agreed, but my voice had run off to Paris without me, apparently.

"I talked with your dad and mom today."

He did what? My head jerked his way so quickly, we almost bonked noses.

"I asked them if I could court you?"

I gulped and whispered, "You did?"

"I did." He gave my hand a squeeze but didn't let go. "He asked if this had to do with the farm, which, when I first thought of it a week and a half ago, it did. And I told him that. I also told him that God's been talking to me, or rather, I'm listening for the first time in my life. I've got to admit, God's been telling me things I never would have imagined. He's been working on my heart. Two weeks ago,

I was a selfish kid. Well, maybe I'm still selfish, but I'm getting better at tuning in to Him."

"And that made you ask if you could court me?" Be still my heart, if Pops gave permission, I'd say "yes" in a heartbeat. Even if he didn't . . . oh, my, I was getting ahead of myself.

"It did. I confessed to God that I was falling for you, and He asked me what I was going to do about it."

Darned if I didn't blush even more.

But the important question was, "What did Momma and Pops say?"

"He asked what my intentions were toward you."

At this, I looked Bernie in the eye, wanting—needing—the truth from him. "What did you tell him?"

He gulped. "I said I'd wasted six years dating without having any intentions other than having a pretty girl at my side. I told him I'm done wasting my time. If I date someone, my intention is marriage."

I laughed hard at that, imagining my parents' faces. "I take it, they booted you out of the house."

He just smiled at me, giving me a look that sent warm shivers over my body.

"They asked if I'd wait one year before getting married."

My only response to that was blinking.

"I said, how about December tenth, since that's the day you saved me from making a mistake with Elaine."

I was still trying to wrap my brain around the fact that they hadn't kicked him out of the house.

"So, what do you say?" And then, he was on the snowy ground, holding up a ring box.

"You're . . . you're proposing?"

"I . . ." His face turned red. "I am."

Joy to the World

"Joy to the World" played lightly in the background as Marlene relived that evening. He'd surprised her, sure enough, and throughout their marriage he'd continued to surprise her. Tonight, she wanted one more surprise: for him to live, really live, through this surgery.

"And?" Tessa leaned toward her, her eyes wide.

Guess she would like to know the rest of the story.

"Mom."

"Ricky?" And Sheila and their two small children. Suzanna always traveled with them, but Matthew often stayed home with his mother. What a delight to have the entire family together.

Marlene closed her eyes and gave thanks for the abundant blessings of family as Ricky knelt and hugged her, leaving his tears on her cheek. Oh, their oldest had given her and Bernie fits, but he'd grown into this amazing man of God. None of that could have happened without the pruning and shaping God had done over the years.

Even when bad things happened, God was still good. And He was always at work, just as He was tonight.

Ricky released his hug but remained kneeling. "How are you doing?"

"God is good, all the time." Yes, it was cliché, but those phrases were birthed for moments like this.

"Yes, yes, He is."

"And I'm surrounded with family." How could she complain?

"More is coming." Her son winked and stood. "Josh, Nate. Help me put these tables together. Food is on the way."

Food? Her stomach growled at the mention. When was the last time she'd eaten? Probably ten or more hours ago, but then, she really hadn't been hungry.

The scent of roast beef entered the room before the meat. Lauren and Jet, Meghan and Doran carried bags of scrumptious-smelling food into the room. Her unofficially adopted children, young adults Marcus and Ricky had mentored over the past years, were just as much a part of the family as those connected by blood.

Her family sat around the table. Minus Bernie. And that broke her heart. Had last year been their final Christmas as a complete family? She refused to accept that.

They gave thanks for the food, prayed for Bernie, the physicians, the medical staff. They prayed for each other. For her.

And then they ate. And laughed. And sang—or tried to sing. They invited hospital staff and others who waited for loved ones to help themselves. Somehow, they had enough to feed all. No, not somehow. God was here. Tonight. And He was good.

“Grandma Marlene?”

She looked to Tessa who sat across from her beside Nathan.

“What did you say to Bernie, when he proposed?” Ah, the child was waiting for the end of the story.

“Yeah, Mom, what did you say?” Marcus smirked, looking so much like his father.

“Well, here’s the story . . .”

I was in shock. Sure, I’d known of Bernie since I started kindergarten, but until two weeks ago, he hadn’t noticed me. To be fair, I hadn’t paid attention to him. Football linebacker? Stupid game. Stupid girls falling all over sports stars in our school. It was all silly.

And now he had to go and show that just because he played football didn’t mean he was shallow and arrogant. He’d proven to be the exact opposite.

But two weeks?

I stared over at his expectant, hope-filled eyes, down at the ring, and then beyond the trees, wondering if *Candid Camera* was filming.

“I . . . I don’t know what to say.”

Some of that hope leaked from his eyes.

Did I love him? I could honestly say, "No," though I did have a major crush on him. Would an engagement solve our problems?

"Did you ask my folks about working on the farm?"

"I did, and your dad said he'd work something out."

"And not sell?"

"That's what it sounded like."

So now, my saying no might cost Bernie his opportunity to farm.

But saying yes went against my better judgment. Bernie deserved better, even if it cost him a job opportunity. Even if Pops sold the farm.

I curved both hands around Bernie's, closing the ring box. "My answer is 'No.' I'm sorry."

He fell back on his bottom in the cold snow and stared at the ground.

"But . . ." I removed my glove and rested my hand on his cheek. That almost felt too forward, even after a proposal. "If your offer to court is still on the table, I'd say an emphatic 'Yes' to that."

"You would?"

I nodded. "And who knows, let's keep December tenth open next year, just in case."

O Come, O Come Emmanuel

"Did you get married the next year?"

Marlene laughed at Tessa's enthusiasm. "We did."

"How did he propose?"

"Hold on." Marlene raised her hand. "There's a little more."

"You made it." Ricky broke in before Marlene could continue her story, and all eyes shot to the hallway where Austin, another of her unofficially adopted grandchildren, helped his very pregnant wife remove her coat.

"Is it time?" Marlene couldn't help but hope, in spite of Dani's due date being three weeks away yet.

Dani shook her head.

"Do you really think Dani would have let us stay home with Grandpa Bernie sick?" Austin squeezed a chair between Ricky and Sheila and helped Dani take a seat.

"We had to be here." Dani reached across the table and took Marlene's hand. "Any news?"

Marlene shook her head. “But if anything will give him motivation to keep fighting, it’s that child you’re carrying.” This would be Bernie’s and her first great-grandson, and nothing thrilled him more, even if there wasn’t a blood or legal connection. This child would be greatly loved. Bernie just had to live through this, so he could hold the boy.

“Then we’ll continue to pray.” Austin glanced around the table, worry narrowing his brows. “Sounds like we interrupted something pretty intense.”

Tessa chimed in. “Only the best part of Marlene and Bernie’s love story. She was just going to tell us about the proposal.”

Marlene laughed, eager to take her mind off of which homecoming Bernie would be celebrating: either his earthly home or his heavenly one. Call her selfish, but she truly hoped she would be celebrating alongside him.

“Well, before he proposed again, he’d promised to court me, so that’s exactly what he did. Oh, he’d take me out for dinner or to a drive-in movie or bowling, ice skating and sledding, but our relationship really grew working alongside each other on the farm. Milking cows, baling straw and hay, scooping manure.”

“Ewww, really?” Tessa cringed. “But what about Paris? Did you ever go?”

“Ah, yes I did, right after Christmas. I stayed with some relatives for a month while exploring every inch of the city, including spending long days touring each art museum Paris has to offer. One day, I even set up my canvas in front of Notre Dame. Oh, it was a glorious month which included Bernie surprising me with a visit during my third week there. Though I'd been to the Louvre more than once, I couldn't wait to go alongside him. It was in front of the Mona Lisa, where he kissed me for the first time."

"Oh, how romantic." Tessa clasped her hands together on the table, her ring in full view, and elbowed her fiancé.

Nathan groaned. "I'd never be able to compete with that."

"Oh, I'm certain you have your own special memories." But that kiss had sure been something special. She sighed just thinking about the moment when her feelings for him became something more, something deeper.

"Did he propose there? Or in front of the Eiffel Tower?"

Marlene shook her head. "Oh, not in Paris, though that would have been lovely, but in the most unexpected place and time."

Despite the waning sunlight, sweat oozed off me as I heaved a bale of hay from the wagon onto the elevator that would carry the bales up the side of the barn and into the hayloft. Bernie and Dad were stacking the hay—letting me work outside rather than in the sweltering barn was the very definition of love. Farming will either separate a couple or bring you together. For us, the seasons of field prep, planting, weeding, harvesting, and a whole heap of praying together only strengthened our love.

If I'd learned one thing these past nine months, it was

that home really was the best place to be, and working alongside Bernie only deepened my love for him. Sure, we'd had our squabbles. I'd learned he had a quick temper, and he experienced more of my childish tantrums. Oh, heavens, I had growing up to do!

I dropped the final bale on the elevator then leaped off the wagon and jogged to the on/off switch on the side of the barn.

A minute later I heard, "Done." Bernie's strong voice came through the window, and I shut off the unit.

I hurried around to the front of the barn where Momma met us with massive bowls of ice cream. I'd learned I could down just as much as the guys after a day's work. Once every drop of ice cream was slurped up, we meandered dirty hand in callused hand to the house, with Rex nudging his way between us. This had become a nightly ritual. Usually, Bernie didn't care how badly I needed a shower when he'd cuddle beside me on the porch swing on the deck and share lingering goodnight kisses. Honestly, I didn't care either.

I did care, though, that December ten was only three months away and Bernie hadn't proposed yet—or again—and I was getting anxious.

With Momma and Pops in the house and the night sky now ruling the day, we climbed up onto the deck and aimed for the swing. Before sitting, Bernie wrapped his arms around my waist and looked me in the eyes, which closed as I awaited his kiss.

But then his arms sprung away and he backed up. "I,

uh, need to get home. See you tomorrow morning for milking." He hurried off the deck and to the pickup he'd bought after selling his El Torino, and he sped off toward home.

What in the world just happened? I stood still, watching the road, waiting for Bernie to come to his senses and return, but the road only grew darker with the night. Numb, I trudged into the house, mumbled "shower" to Momma and Pops. I used up every ounce of hot water, washing the day's work from my hair and my body. Scratches left from hefting hay stung as soap dug in, but at least that made me feel something.

Was I borrowing trouble?

As I dressed for bed, I viewed the top of my bookshelf that showcased Bernie's carvings. The manger scene was nearly complete. Hopefully, for Christmas she could display it beneath the family tree. Was he working on another piece? And what got into him earlier tonight? He hadn't seemed any different. Nothing unusual happened, not until the hasty goodbye. Bernie was anything but hasty—his proposal on Christmas Eve was an anomaly. So, what did that behavior mean now?

I covered a yawn as I crawled beneath my covers. Maybe it meant he was just tired. Yeah, I'd go with that.

My eyes had barely closed when there was a knock on my bedroom door.

"Yeah?" croaked from my scratchy throat.

"It's me." Momma flung open the door. "Cows are out."

No. "Seriously?" I flung off the bedcovers and searched

for my dirty clothes from yesterday.

"They're already in the wash." Momma handed me clean jeans and a T-shirt from my closet. "Meet you downstairs."

Yippee. Just what I needed to end this day. I pulled on my jeans and threw on my bra and shirt and hurried downstairs. Momma met me on the porch and handed me my shoes.

"Pops outside already?" I bent and tied my Keds.

"Uh, yes."

Why the hesitation? Oh, whatever. I'd done enough ruminating tonight to last a lifetime, and those cows wouldn't get back in the cow yard if I didn't focus on my task.

Shoes tied, I hurried outside and aimed for the pasture. Something—rather, someone—grabbed my arm. "What in the world?" My heart started palpitating. I tried shaking them off and opened my mouth to scream.

"Marlene, it's me."

Bernie? My heart calmed and I spun to him as anger rose. "The cows are out. Why aren't you helping Dad?" And why was he here in the first place? I aimed for the pasture and once again, Bernie stopped me.

"The cows aren't out," he said softly.

I blinked and glanced toward the cow yard. The gate was closed. No cows wandered about our yard. What was going on?

"But Momma said—"

He put a finger to my lips and pointed to the northern

sky. My jaw dropped and eyes widened. "Oh . . ."

The master artist was putting on a painting clinic as He feathered his brushes across the night sky, painting it with dancing bright greens, vibrant pinks, and highlighter yellows. Nothing in Paris could ever compare to the Master's hand, and to think He brought His art show to their backyard. Wow!

Bernie nudged my shoulder and offered his arm. "Come with me?"

I studied him with suspicion. A backpack was slung over his shoulders. His hair was clean and neatly combed. No afternoon shadow clung to his face, and a slight scent of aftershave wafted my way. "Where to?"

"It's a surprise."

What did he have up his sleeve? This entire evening was a surprise and an enigma. It had to have something to do with his strange behavior earlier, but suddenly that didn't matter. I'd follow this man anywhere. I took his arm and let him lead me to the barn. He gestured to the silo that rose roughly eighty feet from the ground, and I gulped.

"You game?"

Well, I'd follow him anywhere but there. I glanced upward, studied the ladder surrounded by a metal guard and gulped. Heights scared the bejeebers out of me, but I wasn't about to show Bernie I was a chicken, so I stepped forward, grabbed a rung, and began climbing. My heart rate amped up and my fingers became clammier with each rung. *Lord, help me hang on.*

Bernie climbed right below me, or I might have stopped and headed back down, but there was no stopping now.

"Take deep breaths." His low voice calmed me and soon the excitement of what I was achieving overrode my fear. I'd never had the guts to climb before, not even with Byron's heckling. Oh, if only I'd thought of grabbing a camera to prove my bravery. Ha! I called this bravery when he was over in Nam fighting? No comparison.

After it seemed we'd climbed enough rungs to make it to the top of the Empire State Building, I grasped the silo's concrete top and pulled myself onto the slightly angled roof. I scooted over to make room for Bernie, but that's all the farther I was going. He moved around me and began pulling items from his backpack: a blanket, which he wrapped around my shoulders. I hadn't even realized I was chilled until it draped over goose bumped arms.

He also pulled out a Thermos. "My mom's hot cocoa." He unscrewed the top, filled it, and handed it to me.

I sipped from the Thermos top, and my insides warmed to match the outside as I finally dared to look behind the silo's edge to watch God's paintbrush in motion. "Incredible," I breathed out.

"Isn't it?" He tugged me closer and I leaned into him to watch the art show.

But questions niggled at me. "Is this why you took off so quickly?"

"I'm sorry I was so abrupt." He kissed my temple. "I was about to kiss you goodnight, when I saw the northern lights. I couldn't waste a second."

"You're forgiven."

"I didn't know I was in the doghouse," he said with a smirk.

I punched his arm. "Just don't do it again, buster."

"Yes, ma'am." He pulled something else from his backpack and snuggled even closer.

I was curious about it, but I was even more surprised by a revelation that had just come to me. "Momma lied to me."

"What?" He hid whatever he pulled from the backpack between his legs.

"When she woke me up. She told me the cows were out and that Dad was outside. She never lies."

Bernie raised his hands. "I didn't tell her what to say. I called your place when you were in the shower and explained I wanted to surprise you. It worked. It got you out of bed."

Probably the only thing that would have pulled me from sleep. Momma was forgiven. This time, anyway.

Again, I reclined against Bernie's strong shoulder, and we watched the Aurora Borealis together. He'd been smart bringing me up here where no trees impeded our view.

"I have something else for you." He reached between his legs, pulled out the mystery item, and handed it to her.

I gasped. The last figurine for her manger scene! The wise man holding a box in both hands stood about three inches tall. Oh, it was a beauty.

"Thank you." I looked up at him to thank him with a kiss, but his gaze was on the gift, and his hands nervously ran up and down his thighs. "Is something wrong?"

"Uh, no." His voice cracking, he pointed to the wiseman. "It opens. The gift. It's hinged."

My eyes grew wide as I examined the figure's gift box. I dug my fingernail beneath the lid and, as he'd said, it opened up. And I gasped.

"The wise man carrying gold." I said beneath my breath as I attempted to dig the ring from the box with shaking fingers. I got it out, but then it slipped from my hands and clinked on the concrete roof. "Oh no!" I grasped for it before it took a leap off the side to be gone forever, and missed.

"Have no fear." Grinning, Bernie took the figurine from her, opened the box, and tugged. The ring lifted into the air and deposited into her hand by a fishing wire knotted to the box and the ring.

Clever. "You knew I'd drop it."

"Well, I wanted to have my bases covered just in case." His grin faded and he took the ring from her hand and gripped it between his thumb and forefinger. "When I first proposed, I really didn't understand what love meant. What marriage meant. But these past months have taught me so much about you, about myself. Us. When I visited you in France, I realized then that if you didn't come home, if you'd decided to stay there and pursue your art, I would have joined you. I'd have a booth with vegetables and my carvings, whatever it took to be with you and care for you. The months since then have only deepened that feeling. I will go where God leads me, and that's with you. If you'll be my wife."

Speechless, I stared at the ring. It was a simple gold band with a single diamond, and that fit them perfectly.

"Well?" His voice shook.

"Well, what if I've decided I want to move to France?"

I Heard the Bells on Christmas Day

"You didn't!"

Marlene grinned at Tessa's stunned reaction. "Bernie's reaction was much like yours. Completely stunned. But I had to drag out the romantic evening a little bit. The kiss he gave me when I did say yes made it all worth the wait. And that certainly wasn't the last time we made the climb up to the top of the silo." They'd shared many a sweet moment up there, alone with only God to see them.

Tessa grabbed Nathan's arm. "You never told me your grandparents were so romantic." He just groaned as did many of her family. Most certainly, they were tired of hearing the story every new Brooks family member begged to hear, but Marlene would never tire of telling it.

"We've had our moments." And she desperately wanted those moments to continue. If God chose to let Bernie stay, she wouldn't take any more of their minutes together for granted. "Speaking of moments." Marlene nodded to Tessa and Nathan. "Don't you two have something to say?"

"You're engaged? I saw the ring!" Dani broke in before the young couple had a chance to make their announcement, and she slapped a hand over her mouth. "Sorry. As Austin will tell you, my mouth runs overtime."

The group shared a much-needed laugh and celebrated the engagement. If only Bernie were here to share in this celebration.

"I Heard the Bells on Christmas Day" played lightly over the hospital speakers. A song of grief and a song of hope.

Was it Christmas already? The clock read ten minutes to midnight. Shouldn't surgery be complete by now? The monitor displaying patient progress still read *In Surgery*.

"Let's pray that your father—your grandfather—will continue to share our moments." Fifty years together—life would be so lonely without him.

It shouldn't be. She glanced around the waiting room filled with family. Perhaps "lonely" wasn't the right word. She'd never be lonely, but she'd be missing a part of herself, and that pruning would be excruciating.

"Marlene Brooks?" She turned toward the unfamiliar voice. The surgeon! She leaped up and felt her family gather around her.

"Would you like to speak in private?" Dr. Packer wore a poker face as he gestured toward an office.

Please God. I know I said Your will be done, but I'm not ready to lose Bernie.

She felt tears escape her eyes as she shook her head. "I

would prefer to hear the news surrounded by family."

The doctor offered a weary smile at that. "You are blessed with family."

"Yes." She felt hands rest on her shoulders. "Yes I am."

"Then shall we at least sit down?" He didn't wait for an answer but led the way to the tables where they'd shared supper. The entire family sat in wary silence.

"Your husband is a strong man, Mrs. Brooks, with severely blocked arteries."

All that she already knew. "And?"

He removed his glasses, wiped them, put them back on. "There were a couple of times we thought we were losing him."

She blinked. Did that mean he'd made it?

"We could all tell your prayer warriors were working overtime."

"Dr. Packer." No surprise, Marcus was clearly impatient. "Just get to the point. How is our father?"

The man smiled. "Your father is . . ." He turned to Marlene. "Your husband came through surgery. We were able to clear the arteries, and unless something unexpected happens, he should fully recover."

"Praise God." Marlene whispered the prayer, but her family wasn't nearly so silent. One would think their favorite team won the championship game.

Perhaps it had.

"But."

One little word from the doctor silenced the throng.

"He has to make changes in his diet."

That she knew.

"And exercise more."

That too.

"And most of all, keep praying."

"We never stop, doctor. You and your team were lifted up."

"We always appreciate the help." He nodded to the family. "Oh, and one more thing."

One more? Oh, her heart couldn't take any more. She'd be on the operating table next.

Dr. Packer pointed to the clock hanging by the vending machines, showing 12:01 AM. "Merry Christmas."

The sentiment was echoed around the room and then they each bowed their heads and gave thanks for the Child who became their Savior.

This was definitely a Christmas homecoming to remember.

Read more about Marlene and Bernie Brooks's family in Brenda S. Anderson's *Coming Home Series*.

The Coming Home Series

Pieces of Granite
Chain of Mercy
Memory Box Secrets
Hungry for Home

Plus Novelettes in Mosaic Collection Anthologies:

A Christmas Homecoming –
A Novelette in *A Star Will Rise*
Coming Home – a Novelette in *All Things New*
The Home for Christmas Challenge –
A Novelette in *A Thrill in the Air*

A Note from the Author

Since completing the *Coming Home Series* back in 2015, I've always wanted to explore the romance between the heads of Brooks family, Marlene and Bernie. In this Christmas short story, I finally had an opportunity, and it surprised me. I loved getting to know the piece of the Brooks family history in this stand-alone story, and I hope you enjoyed it, too.

If you haven't read my *Coming Home Series*, I recommend beginning with *Pieces of Granite*, the prequel.

I hope you have a very blessed Christmas!

~ Brenda

COMPANION SHORT STORY TO
A BEAUTIFUL MESS

A BEAUTIFUL Christ-mess

BRENDA S. ANDERSON

A BEAUTIFUL CHRIST-MESS

Companion Short Story to
A Beautiful Mess

When prodigal son Zachary Belden returns home at Christmas to surprise his family with news, he's stunned by other news that turns his surprise into a big mess and challenges his newfound faith.

This story originally appeared in
The Mosaic Collection's 2019 Christmas anthology,
Hope is Born.

Dedication

To my amazing and very large family:

Our Christmases are frequently messy,
but always beautiful!

Chapter One

Sunday, December 1, 2019

After spending months overseas, Zachary Belden couldn't wait to get home. His news was the best gift he could give his parents—his entire family!—for Christmas, and he was eager to deliver it.

Whistling "Jingle Bells," Zax strode through the Minneapolis-St. Paul airport, his camera bag slung over his shoulder. Normally, his arriving home three weeks before Christmas would be surprise enough, but what he had to tell them would likely bring on tears. Even from his dad. So much had happened in the four months since he'd last seen them.

He stepped outside, and the cold air slapped him. Thankfully, it wasn't snowing too. Was it only yesterday he was basking in Israel's sixty-five degrees? The seventeen-hour flight made it seem longer. His eagerness to arrive home also played a part in the flight's perceived length.

Regardless, he was on Minnesota soil now, and in about three hours, he'd arrive at his parents' just in time for their Sunday supper.

He spotted his rideshare, a red Ford Escape, zigzagging between three rows of vehicles picking up those who'd just arrived. He jogged toward it while confirming the make, model, color, and license plate of the car with his app. Check.

A woman, probably in her late twenties, stepped out of the SUV and offered her hand. "Zachary Belden?"

"That's me."

"I'm Stephenie Winter."

"Nice to meet you, Stephenie." They shook hands. So, she knew his name and correctly identified herself. A couple more safety checks.

"And I'm taking you to . . ." She tapped at her phone then read off his North Loop, Minneapolis address, an apartment he shared with a friend.

"You've got it." One more check. He'd learned you could never be too careful.

"Perfect." She popped open the hatch.

Grunting, he lifted his overweight suitcase and laid it in the back with a thunk. Not living out of a suitcase for a month would sure be nice. Sleeping in his own bed wouldn't be a hardship either.

He got in the backseat, passenger side of the vehicle, and buckled in.

"Do you have a preferred route?" She looked in the

rearview mirror as she buckled.

"Whichever way is fastest." He'd waited long enough to spring his surprise.

"Gotcha." She nodded, pulled out into the driving lane, and took off. So, she had a little bit of a lead foot. If that got him home sooner, all the better.

He stretched out the kinks in his back and neck from the flight while observing Stephenie in the mirror. Long, silky chestnut hair topped with a Minnesota Vikings stocking cap. Caramel eyes. Full lips. Would it hurt to ask her out?

Seriously, dude? He shook his head. This new lifestyle he'd vowed to live was going to be a lot harder than he imagined. But God had his back. Finally, he'd taken that to heart. To avoid temptation, he closed his eyes and imagined his folks' reaction when he told them his news. But first he had to stop at his apartment, drop off his suitcase, pick up his Camaro, and then make the two-plus-hour trip up to Brainerd.

Even that seemed like forever away.

He opened his eyes and watched vehicles and homes whiz past on familiar roads that welcomed him home with snow-filled ditches and white-tipped trees.

A wave of sadness swept through him. Had it already been over seven months since his younger brother went to be with Jesus? A freak April blizzard. A car crash. A—

The car braked and skidded, fishtailing, and he gripped the door handle as the vehicle sailed toward the ditch. His sorry life playing in front of his eyes, he braced himself as the crossover plowed into the ditch. It jerked to a stop in a drift that reached to his window.

He breathed out a sigh. They were stuck, but alive. That was more than he could say for Corey.

Stephenie looked back at him, grimacing. "Sorry about that. I didn't expect that guy to be going so slow."

Well, if you weren't going twenty miles over the speed limit, maybe you could have stopped. Zax gritted his teeth before those words exited his mouth.

"I'll get help." She whipped out her phone.

Right. He knew how long that help would take to arrive. Guess that would be her problem. He brought up the ride share app and requested a new ride. They'd be here in ten minutes. Perfect.

"A tow should arrive in about an hour." She shrugged as if it were no big deal.

"My new ride will be here in ten." He shrugged back.

"Seriously?" Her gaze met his in the mirror. "I thought maybe you and I could, you know, go out for a drink later."

Talk about brazen. It was like looking at himself—his former self—in the mirror.

"Sorry, but I'm taken." Maybe he skirted the truth a bit, but that line usually got the flirts to back down.

"I won't tell if you won't."

Oh, brother. He didn't answer, just shook his head, and closed his eyes. His life's mirror was not being friendly today.

Next thing he heard was the hatch being popped open. Had he fallen asleep? His ride must be here.

"You getting out or not?"

He stared at her in the mirror. Those dark eyes said she wasn't kidding. He didn't even try his door; the snow was packed so high against it. The door behind the driver wasn't any better, which meant he had to suck it up and crawl out the back.

He lowered the back of the seat beside him, slung his camera bag around his arm and neck, and crept out of the crossover.

And sunk knee-deep into snow. He dragged his suitcase from the back and tried to climb out of the ditch while pulling it, but its weight sunk him further.

He heard a clonk as the hatch closed behind him. What a piece of work she was.

Shivering, he glanced to his left. Nothing but other vehicles flying past. Nothing to his right either. Score one for Stephenie. His review would not be complimentary.

He high-stepped through the snow, to the shoulder of the road, where he set down his camera, then he trudged back to the crossover and dragged his suitcase up the short embankment. Even in the cold, he was sweating.

Good thing he was going home to change before heading up north.

He tugged his suitcase further away from the Ford, creating several cars' distance between him and his ride, then used it as a chair.

The wind whipped through his now-wet sweatshirt and jeans, chapping his body, and numbing his fingers. Sure, he had a suitcase full of clothes, but nothing that would stand up to a Minnesota winter. After checking his ride app to see that his driver was still four minutes out, he rubbed his hands in front of his mouth and blew on them, then stuck his frozen fingers beneath his armpits.

What seemed like an hour later, a massive SUV rolled off the highway and stopped right behind Zax. The license plate matched the app information, as did the vehicle type. Although, right now, Zax would likely take a ride from anyone who didn't look like a masked murderer.

Or another woman looking for an easy date.

A Paul Bunyan lookalike, with his long beard and red-and-black checkered shirt, stepped from the SUV. The face matched the app's picture. "Get yourself ditched, Zachery Belden?" The man laughed heartily at his own joke.

"You could say that." Zax murmured through his frozen lips as he stood and carefully unbent his fingers. He tried grasping his suitcase handle, but his fingers wouldn't cooperate.

"Let me give you a hand with that." The man lifted the suitcase as if it were filled with marshmallows. "By the way, my name's Paul Dickson." He set the suitcase in the back of the vehicle.

"Zax." He stretched out his arm, but his fingers still didn't want to work.

"Zax, it is." Paul opened the back door. "Climb on in. Let's get you warmed up. Got you some hot cocoa there, too."

"Bless you." The strange words spilled from Zax's mouth, although they did fit the occasion.

The vehicle pulled onto the freeway, and Zax smiled through thawing lips and waved at Stephenie. For some reason, she didn't return the favor.

"Girlfriend issues?"

Zax snorted and said in between shivers, "Driver issues. She made a pass at me. I told her to keep on truckin'."

The man guffawed. "Well, I can promise you, you won't have to worry about that from me. My wife might take an issue with that."

"Much appreciated." As was the hot chocolate. Zax curled both hands around the mug, slowly thawing them at the same time the drink warmed his insides.

Twenty minutes later, Zax was up in his apartment changing. And then showering to remove the days' worth of travel stench frozen to his body. Although he wouldn't have minded talking to his roommate, the man didn't know how to shut up. The ride had already set him back about an hour, and he didn't want to waste any more time. Still, he should arrive at his childhood home early for supper.

Real, homemade food. Made by his mom, the best cook in the Midwest. Nah, he wasn't biased.

Just the thought of the meal made his mouth water and his stomach growl, and that propelled him out the door even faster.

He hurried to the underground garage and his red Camaro. It looked clean and sharp, as he hadn't driven it in months. Of course, in winter, the clean wouldn't last a foot past the garage exit. Zax preferred not taking it out on the salty winter roads, but right now he didn't have a choice. Someday he'd be smart and buy a junker just for winter.

He squealed out of the garage—he just couldn't help himself, having not driven his precious car for months—onto city streets which had been turned off-white by a salt mix used to make the road less slick. Still, years of driving in Minnesota winters—and riding with Stephenie—had taught him that slick spots remained.

Sort of like life.

Oh, now he was going all philosophical. Snap out of it, dude!

With Christmas music playing from his radio app playlist, he wove his way through the city streets until he was on I-94 heading north. It wasn't long before he turned off onto a state highway going northwest. There was something calming about driving these familiar roads. As much as he loved traveling, coming home eased tension he didn't realize he'd been feeling.

Before long, he turned off that freeway onto another road, the last stretch before home. It should only take him thirty-five minutes or so. Supper was usually served at five on Sundays, giving him a half hour to spare. He could smell his mom's cooking already. Apparently, his stomach did too, as it growled in anticipation.

He passed between two rows of pines, and the sunset in his rearview mirror yanked his attention. Wow! The sun was arcing down where the trees made way for the road, as if the forest had split especially for the sun's descent. That was beautiful enough, but the vivid colors God was painting with were breathtaking. No doubt, his brother Corey was wielding a brush right alongside Jesus at this very moment.

Zax slowed. He had time yet to snap a few pics to add to his online gallery.

But he really wanted to get home.

But his nieces would be upset if he saw one of their dad's works and didn't stop to capture it. That compelled him to pull off, carefully, onto the ice-covered shoulder. His nieces could compel him to do most anything.

He grabbed his camera, got out of the car, and planted himself behind the vehicle. Looking through the viewfinder, he shook his head. This angle didn't work. He needed to get higher. And quickly. Once the sun decided to set, it didn't dally.

Problem was, going higher meant climbing up on his car. With snow boots.

His car's pristine finish or his nieces' smiles?

No competition.

Wincing, he climbed up on the trunk and aimed the camera. Still not right, so he stepped up on the roof. At least he'd been smart and not bought a convertible, though when he'd bought the used vehicle as a teen, he'd really wanted one.

The view from the roof was perfection. He snapped shots in rapid succession as the sun slid between the trees, coloring the skies with brilliant purple, orange, and red.

Yeah, Corey had to be apprenticing today. His brother had loved bright colors.

As the sun was about to disappear, Zax laid the camera against his chest and watched. He loved seeing the last blink of the day. Watching the sun descend over the Sea of Galilea had brought tears to his eyes more than once.

Just like that, the sun disappeared.

But that didn't make the colors reflected from the clouds any less magnificent. With travelers whizzing past, he sat on the roof of his car, transfixed by God's paintbrush in motion, not caring about the air temperatures dropping as quickly as the sun had. He raised his hands in praise of the One Who welcomed home prodigals with stunning gifts such as this.

What had Zax ever done to deserve this love?

Nothing, he knew. That was the thing about grace: it was undeserved. After thirty-plus years of that lesson being drummed into his brain, his heart finally listened along with it.

He glanced at his watch and winced. There went all his margin time. Now he'd arrive home as the meal was being served. Still not bad planning, but he'd hoped to get in some conversation before they sat to eat.

Suddenly feeling the brunt of the cold air, he slid from the top of the car, got in, and turned the heat on full blast. Ahhh, nothing like modern technology. He held his fingers against the vents for a few minutes, helping unthaw them again, before steering back onto the road.

Prudence kept him from going fast. Not only were there

slick spots on the road, but at this time of night, deer that had survived hunting season loved venturing out into traffic, playing chicken with vehicles. They usually materialized out of forests and pranced their way onto the road at the very moment vehicles passed.

Better to take it slow and arrive home in one piece than to contribute to Minnesota's roadkill population. Besides, his parents would be devastated if they lost both sons in less than a year. He couldn't do that to them.

His radio app must have heard his thoughts as Burl Ives' version of "Rudolph, the Red-Nosed Reindeer" began playing. Zax couldn't resist singing along, including the childhood additions he had to make certain to teach his youngest niece, Clara, his brother's youngest daughter.

Bright headlights crested the hill in front of him, and he flicked his own headlights off and on, hoping they'd take the hint and dim theirs. Something flashed ahead on the side of the road, and Zax stomped on the brakes. His car spun a full donut, and he yelled out, "Help me, Jesus!" before coming to a stop on the side of the road, facing the wrong direction. The high-beamed vehicle zoomed on down the road without slowing, the—

He flung a curse name at the driver, then lifted up a quick apology to God. Boy, did he have a long way to go in his walk of faith. Old habits really were hard to change.

His heart beat faster than the other car had fled. But he wasn't in the ditch. Like Stephenie. That made him chuckle. That the other vehicle hadn't hit him was a blessing. For that he was thankful.

He looked in the rearview mirror, and a ten-point buck stood in the middle of the road, his head held high as if gloating. Zax could just hear it thinking, *Na, na, na, na, na, na. I survived deer-hunting season, and I can survive crossing the road, too.*

The arrogant buck leaped away. Zax would love to see the animal become venison stew.

His heart rate slowing, he turned his car in the right direction, then pulled onto the shoulder. Before driving, he needed to be completely calm. Who knew driving home from the airport would be such an adventure? He'd had more close calls on this drive than he'd had during his last months of retracing the apostle Paul's journeys for a photojournalism assignment.

Well, not completely true. His heart had undergone a spiritual transplant on that journey. His folks were going to be thrilled. They'd be just as excited with his other news, too.

His nerves finally settling, he pulled onto the road, heading north. By now, his folks would be seated at the supper table, with whomever they'd decided to invite for the day. They rarely ate by themselves. How had he not seen Jesus working through them when he was growing up? Now, His light was far brighter than any vehicle's high beams.

It had taken years, but Zax had at last seen God's light and run to it. Just like he was running toward home right now.

Twenty minutes later, with his family probably halfway

through supper, Zax pulled onto the road he'd grown up on. It was paved now, but that occurred after he'd left home. Before then, it had been gravel, and as kids, they'd called it a boom-boom road. Back then he hadn't appreciated having a lake in his back yard. In this area of Minnesota, that wasn't uncommon. Traveling through hundreds of miles of deserts had opened his eyes to how rare lakes were.

A handful of homes away, his house came into view. At Christmastime, it was always easy to spot. His parents never overdid the Christmas light thing: just a single line of very straight white lights bordering the roof line. A tree strung with multicolored lights was centered in the front room window. Every year it was the same—there was something calming about that unchanging familiarity.

Three vehicles sat in the driveway. He squinted, trying to guess who would be there. The minivan was probably Erin's, his brother's ex-wife. Or was she his widow now that Corey had passed? The sedan, that was likely Jon Monson's, a childhood friend who was about to marry Erin. On Christmas Day, of all days, and in Jon's lakeside home. Zax never would have guessed Erin would go for such a thing as being married on a holiday—she was so pragmatic and never made decisions based on emotion. Maybe they figured that would get him home for the season.

Guess they were right. Although, this year, he'd planned on coming home anyway.

The third vehicle in the driveway was very familiar. It

both surprised and excited him.

A pink pick-up.

No one but Gina Holmquist, Jon's legal assistant, would have a pink pick-up. It fit her personality perfectly.

So, he would get to see her again, much sooner than he'd planned. They'd dated whenever he was in town, the last time being four months ago. Back then, he'd been thinking maybe she would be the one to pry him from his bachelor life.

He still had to apologize for his behavior before he left town. He was no longer that man. Apparently, God was making certain Zax would get in that apology.

He parked on the street and puffed out a breath. Seeing his parents was one thing, but knowing he'd see Gina again so soon unnerved him in a way he hadn't expected. He'd cared for her more than anyone else he'd dated. But now, dating anyone was out of the question.

Steeling himself, he grabbed his camera bag from the passenger seat and strode toward his home, the front door decorated with a red-bowed wreath.

He tried the front door. Unlocked, which wasn't unusual. Slowly, he turned the knob and pushed open the door, hoping it wouldn't squeal and announce his visit. Knowing his dad's penchant for using WD-40 though, Zax would have been surprised if the door made a noise a mouse could hear. He stepped inside the foyer and shut the door as quietly as he'd opened it, all the while listening for voices down the hallway. Talking. Laughter. Clara's cherubic voice mixed with Mik's now-common whine. Ah, puberty. He didn't envy Erin and Jon the season they were about to go through with Erin's daughter—who was also Corey's daughter.

Nothing in their conversation indicated they'd heard him enter.

Good.

The scent of roast beef made his taste buds water. Oh, man, nothing smelled as good as Mom's roast. And it tasted even better.

He quickly removed his shoes and set them on the mat beside the door and hung his jacket in the coat closet. Then he tiptoed in stocking feet past the front room his family rarely used, and followed his nose down the short hallway. The oak-strip floors were still kept impeccably shiny by his mom. Ahead was a picture window showcasing barren oaks, green pines, and the lake, now frozen over. The temperatures this year had been extra cold, so he and his dad could probably get in some ice fishing. He couldn't wait to tell his dad about other fishing he'd been doing, and would be doing in the future.

He stopped at the end of the hallway, just before it spilled into the living area. Kitchen and dining room to the left. Family room to the right, with a four-season porch extending toward the lake. Windows stretched the length of the home, offering a panoramic view, which was magnificent in any season.

Stop stalling, dude. Just step out, brace your knees for hugs from Clara. He peeked around the corner at the dining table and almost felt like crying. This was his family. People who loved him, no matter what.

"Uncle Zax!" Mik screeched and pushed back her chair. It fell over as she ran to him, but that didn't slow her as she barreled into his arms. "I've missed you so much!"

"Hey, Mik." He kissed the teen's forehead. "I've missed you, too."

"Unca Zax." Clara, Corey's daughter from his second marriage, who was now being raised by Erin, Corey's ex-wife—talk about a complicated family tree!—struggled to be released from her chair. Everyone else stood, each calling out their own greeting.

All except for Gina. Her gaze avoided his.

What was up with that?

Whatever. Right now, he planned to soak up the love from his family. Even Erin gave him a hug, and she was your classic non-hugger.

Before he barely had time to blink, another place setting was squeezed in between Jon and Gina, who'd managed to give him what looked like a nervous smile. His plate overflowed with beef, mashed potatoes, gravy, corn, and homemade rolls. All his favorites. He couldn't have asked for a better *welcome home* meal. He took one bite of the roast beef, and his eyes rolled back in his head. Oh, man, this had to be served at the heavenly table.

"Good?" his mom asked.

He moaned his appreciation, which made her smile.

"I haven't tasted anything this good for four months when Dad grilled burgers." Why his dad's burgers tasted better than anywhere else, he didn't know, but they did.

"Will you be staying here?" His mom passed the meat tray, probably seeing that he'd devoured his helping already.

"A few nights at least." He heaped more meat onto his plate. "I've got to finish a project and all my equipment's in my apartment, but I'll be in and out until the wedding." He looked to his dad. "And I'd love to toss a line with you a time or two. I'm craving a good sunny or crappie."

His dad wiped a napkin over his mouth, probably covering his big grin. "I s'pose I could manage a day or two off, if your mother will let me."

"Is tonight soon enough?" His mom gestured toward the lake. "Word has it the fish are biting."

They all laughed. Conversation continued around the table until everyone was full, and the table was magically cleaned off. Zax never did understand how that happened.

He also didn't understand the silence coming from the normally talkative and enthusiastic Gina. He was sitting right beside her, yet she'd barely said a word to him, barely smiled at him. She spent more time staring at her plate, and moving food around with her fork.

"Anyone have room for dessert?" Mom came from the kitchen carrying a pie.

Erin brought plates, forks, and ice cream.

"Apple?" His mouth drooled.

"Your favorite." She set it on the table.

Oh, man. It was as if she'd anticipated him coming home. First his favorite meal, now his favorite pie.

Maybe now was a good time to bring up his big news.

It'd be the cherry on top of the day. "Before we dig in, I have a little surprise for you all."

His dad had been halfway through cutting the pie and drew back. "More of a surprise than you coming home early?"

"Yes." Gina beat him to the answer. "A much bigger, better surprise."

His head whiplashed toward her. Now she talked?

She stood.

And his mouth dropped open. Whoa. The normally slender Gina was no longer slim. Oh, she wasn't fat, but a baby bump was obvious. He swallowed hard as she looked down at him and nodded then motioned for him to stand.

On robotic legs, he obeyed. Not knowing if he should smile or what, he watched her for the lead.

She took his hand and raised them together, and his mouth went dry as cotton. On her left hand, there was a ring. An engagement ring. So, why was she holding *his* hand if she was engaged and obviously pregnant with the man's child?

More fear than happiness shone from her eyes as she looked up at him and smiled, telling him he should keep following her lead.

"Zax and I are . . ." Her eyes bore into it, seeming to beg him. Then she raised her chin, as if she were gaining confidence. "Well, as you all know, I'm pregnant." Uncomfortable chuckles came from his family. And him. "So Zax and I, we're going to get married."

Say what?

Zax did his best to rein in his shock, but instead, forced a smile everyone probably saw through and shrugged his shoulders. “Surprise?”

Chapter Two

Surprise? That was all Zax could manage? Not, uh-uh, no way, this isn't my child. That would be an impossibility. But instead, he stood there, dumbfounded, wearing a stupid, fake grin as disingenuous congratulations echoed around the table. Obviously, they were as shocked as he. He wrapped his arm around the woman he thought he knew. Apparently not.

This was the first of December, not April Fool's.

And then there were the looks accompanying his family's fake well-wishes. His dad shaking his head in disappointment. His mom blinking away unhappy tears. His niece rolling her eyes at adults who didn't know how to behave. Erin just stood there, a blank look on her face, one he knew meant she was processing the information. And Jon, he clearly wasn't happy, but his gaze was measured toward Gina.

What just happened here?

Could he rewind the clock five minutes, prevent Gina from standing, so he could make his surprise announcement that his family would be honestly happy for?

Until he knew what she was up to, he decided to play along with her. He wrapped both arms around her and kissed her cheek, then whispered, "You don't leave until we talk."

She nodded and kissed him back. The kiss of good friends, not lovers.

Before they talked, though, he needed to be all prayed up because his thoughts right now said he pretty much wanted to strangle her.

The joy that had earlier surrounded the meal was now muted. Even his apple pie was tainted with Gina's proclamation. But he ate it anyway. And had seconds. He couldn't let it go to waste.

And then came the guests' slow procession home.

At the door, Erin offered him her sincere congratulations. "You'll be a good father," she told him while putting on her winter coat.

"The best," Jon added drily, not masking his lawyer-face at all as he picked up nearly four-year-old Clara. The guy was ticked.

Zax wanted to explain, but his gut told him to remain quiet. Why would God want him silent?

"We're talking. Soon." Jon said under his breath then walked out the door with his future family.

"Uh, yeah. Just give me a call." Zax's mouth went dry,

wondering if Jon's version of "talk" was a fist to the eye. He'd done that to Corey when his brother cheated on and divorced Erin. Corey had deserved it. A few years back, a threat from Jon was just hot air, but now the guy had bulked up and could probably take Zax.

Seven months earlier, when Zax first dated Gina, Jon had warned him not to hurt her. He couldn't deny that he'd hurt her three months later when he'd returned to his overseas project, but they hadn't slept together. Ever.

He gulped and debated escaping or rejoining his family. All that remained were his folks, him, and Gina, who was helping his mom clean. But escaping was what he used to do. He was a changed man. Too bad his family didn't know the truth.

Unfortunately, the truth would be less believable to his family than Gina's lie. Speaking of which, he couldn't wait any longer to hear her story. He had to interrupt meal clean-up and find out what had possessed the slightly quirky, usually intelligent woman.

He strode into the kitchen and kissed his mother's cheek. "Mind if I borrow my . . ." He cleared his throat. *Say it, dude.* "My fiancée for a bit." He practically gagged on the word.

"Oh, not at all." His mom took the drying towel from Gina, who excused herself to go to the bathroom. "You two need some time together. Your father and I will head up to our room."

"Appreciate it."

She patted his cheek and whispered, "I have a feeling

you were just as surprised by this as we were, but we do know that there's nothing more beautiful than raising a child."

"I hope so." As long as it's your own child. "Tell Gina I'm in the four-season room. Gotta do some praying."

"I'll do that."

He headed for the porch.

"Wait. Did you say, 'praying'?"

He turned back, and his smile was genuine this time. "That was gonna be my surprise." Well, the first one, anyway.

She hurried to him and embraced him in a hug, making him want to cry. Then she stepped back, looked up at him, and held his face in her hands. "Then everything will be okay."

"I hope you're right." He walked away from her to the porch, picturing Jesus already there waiting to talk. God was always ready with a listening ear.

Zax didn't sit or kneel or fold his hands. That wasn't how they conversed the best. Rather he looked out the window, held up his hands, palms skyward, and whispered, "What went wrong?"

He closed his eyes, shutting out the world's chaos, and tried listening, but clutter in his brain squirreled through his thoughts, not allowing him to hear God's voice. But still, he stood there, listening.

"Are you okay?"

Startled, he turned to Gina. Her face was blotchy, and her eyes red. No surprise, she'd been crying.

"I should be asking that of you." His gaze traveled to the kitchen, dining room, and family room. All were empty.

"They went to bed." She hugged herself above the baby bump. "Giving us space."

He nodded, then gestured toward a loveseat. He sat on one end, and she took the other and didn't try to stop her tears.

What could he say without adding to her obvious grief? Small talk? "How far along are you?"

"Four months," she said to her lap.

Four months would fit right into the timeline of when he was last in the States. That didn't help his case any.

"Gina, I don't understand. What's going on?" he said as gently as possible, wanting to reach over and comfort her with a touch, but he didn't want to give her any idea that he planned to go along with this cockamamie scheme of hers.

"It's not yours."

"Oh, really? And here I thought since it's almost Christmas, there was another immaculate concept . . ." He bit his tongue, far too late. "I'm sorry. That was uncalled for."

"Not any more uncalled for than a surprise baby and engagement." Her hands did a wringing dance in her lap. "But I saw you, and that's all I could think of."

"How about, 'I'm having a baby. The bio-dad is out of the picture.' Is that a correct assumption?"

She nodded. "Thanks to Jon."

"So, he knows."

"He drew up the paperwork."

Zax splayed his hands. "I don't get it. Why not just say that?"

She cradled her hands around her stomach. "Because I don't want him growing up without a dad. I want him to grow up knowing that men are good, that they don't hurt their girlfriends—"

"He did what?" Zax bolted off the loveseat. "Where is the . . ." He used a word he'd banished from his vocabulary.

"He didn't hit me."

"Did he . . ." Rape you? Zax's gaze went to her stomach then to her face.

She shook her head. "No. No he didn't. After you went back overseas, after you ignored my advances, I returned to him, forgetting what a loser he was."

Zax paced the room, his hands entwined behind his neck. Their last night together before he returned to his job had been an evening of flirting and some heavy making out. Somehow, before things went too far, he'd grown a conscience. If he hadn't, would Gina be in this predicament?

He stopped pacing and looked down at her. "I still don't understand what this has to do with me."

"Please, sit." She patted the loveseat.

He sat as far from her as he could. "I'm listening." That was what God would want him to do, right?

"I love your family." She stared out into the family room. On the wall above the couch, Mom had hung his and

Corey's high school graduation pictures. By then, Zax had already gotten into his share of trouble. Corey didn't mess up until he'd been married to Erin for a number of years. But they were both screw-ups.

"Our messed-up family?"

"Maybe so, but you love each other fiercely. I want that—I *need* that for my son."

"But you can't just announce it and make it so. I like you, Gina, a lot, and if circumstances were different, I would have considered pursuing a relationship. But not this way. It can't happen." Besides, even if he wanted to marry Gina, he could never be a father or a husband, not when he'd made a vow to God to commit his life to Him.

"You won't think about it? Just a little bit?" She showed him the sexy pout thing she excelled at that had once made his gut swirl.

Attraction did not equal a lifetime commitment. "There's nothing to think about. I'm sorry."

She reached over and touched his hand. "For the time being, can we keep it quiet? So your family doesn't think I'm a flake?"

If that was what it took to satisfy her. "I suppose."

"Promise me?"

"I can't tell anyone?"

"Promise."

"Fine."

"Pinky swear?" She held up her hand.

He shook his head and hooked pinkies. "Pinky swear." Years ago, when he'd hung out with Corey, Erin, and Jon, "pinky swear" was an unbreakable promise. Guess it still was.

"And maybe while you're in town, you and I could do supper or catch a movie?"

"As long as you realize that a date doesn't equal engagement or that I'm looking for more."

She held out her hand. "It's a deal."

Instead of shaking, he kissed her on the cheek. This was not a business transaction, and he wouldn't treat it as such.

"You may not realize it, Zachary, but you're easy to love."

He grinned. "That's not what my mom tells me."

She caressed her stomach and stood up. "Little one and I need to head home. Jon still expects me to show up at work tomorrow."

"The slave driver." He walked with her to the front door.

"Oh, I know. Won't let me take a day off to do my nails, and I've chewed them to the nub with this pregnancy."

"Well, he better get his priorities straight." He found her coat in the closet and helped her put it on. "I'll walk you out."

"Thank you."

After she put on her coat, scarf, and gloves, he walked her to her pink pickup and helped her climb in. With her seated, he stood eye to eye with her. She was an attractive woman, no doubt about that, and if things were different, if God hadn't called him to the mission field, maybe he would have turned her announcement into the truth.

But that was a lot of "maybes" to overcome.

"We'll be in touch," he said, then closed her pickup door.

He watched her drive off, then expelled a long breath. What had he just gotten himself into? Like the apostle Paul, God was calling him to spread the gospel, and like Paul, he planned to do it single.

Zax hurried back into the house. Like a dummy, he'd gone outside without a winter coat. That would not happen again.

His mother met him at the door with a hot cocoa, probably her homemade concoction. Oh, she knew him well.

"Come join us." She gave a sideways nod to the front room. That meant they were about to have a talk. Every time he messed up, this was where his parents doled out his punishment, probably because views of the lake couldn't distract anyone.

He followed her into the room, feeling like that young boy who'd been misbehaving. That had happened a lot. Oh, he'd been a tester from the beginning, but they had loved him through it all.

His dad was seated on the couch and his mom sat alongside. He took the wing chair that was placed directly opposite the couch.

"About tonight." He focused on the painting above the couch, one of the last watercolors Corey had created before his untimely death. "I know you're disappointed."

"At least you're taking responsibility." His dad's voice boomed.

"Yeah, something like that." Zax brushed his fingers through his hair, wishing he hadn't promised Gina not to tell anyone. Here he was, actually innocent, and he wasn't able to let his parents know the truth. "But there's more to my story." He wasn't going to spill Gina's secret, but he needed to tell them about his time in Israel.

Dad took Mom's hand, a signal that they planned to listen without interruption.

"Mom knows this part already." Zax took a breath then made a point of looking directly in first his mom's eyes, then his dad's. "I met Jesus this fall."

His dad looked to the ceiling and whispered something. His mom closed her eyes and nodded as if having a private conversation with God.

He scooted to the edge of his chair, closing the distance between them. "As you know, I've been working on this piece called *Walking Through the New Testament*, told from a secular perspective. With every step, Jesus dogged me. He was there alongside me, insisting I believe He existed, that He was . . . *is* the Son of God. That He died to save me. And I could no longer deny that He rose from the grave. Not only does the Bible tell us this, but historical evidence proves it. And then, watching Corey over his last years of life, messing up with Erin, then turning his life around, I just couldn't deny it."

His mom sobbed softly, and his dad wrapped an arm around her back. "Was that your real surprise?"

"That was part A."

"Part A?" Mom asked.

Zax nodded and then relayed part B, which would probably shock them more. “God’s called me to the mission field, and I’ve been offered a job starting after the new year.”

Chapter Three

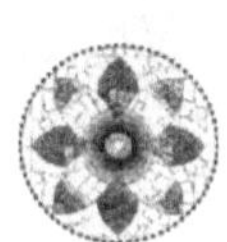

Now he really had stunned his parents into silence. They were less shocked when Gina announced the false engagement.

"Are you sure about this, Zachary?"

Zachary. Mom's way of asserting the fact that she indeed was his mother.

She folded her hands in her lap, probably to help herself remain calm. "Just how do you know this is your path?"

"I talk with God. All the time."

"And you listen?" This from his father, who hadn't always demonstrated the best listening skills.

"Of course."

"Well then, we need to offer you our full support." His dad spread open his hands. "However, you need it. Prayer goes without saying. But financial. Emotional. Whatever you require, son."

"That means a lot to me. Thank you."

"And Gina's agreed to go with you?"

"I, uh . . ." He scratched his head. "We're still working on the logistics."

"Well, I must say, you've given our hearts a lot of jolts tonight." His dad slapped his thighs. "And I'm tuckered out. We've got a busy day tomorrow, a busy month ahead, so I need my beauty rest." He winked at Zax's mom, who rolled her eyes. That was probably where Mik, his niece, learned it from.

Zax watched the two climb the stairs to their bedroom, then sank back in the chair. At least his parents knew his plans. The problem now was, what was he supposed to do or say about Gina?

Zax's alarm awoke him far too early the next morning. This traveling across multiple time zones was getting more difficult the older he got, so the sooner he adjusted to his new time, the better.

He got up, showered and shaved, then hurried downstairs, hoping to catch some hot breakfast. Mom was setting the table, and Dad was pulling something out of the oven.

"Johnny cake?" His taste buds began salivating again. By the time he flew back overseas, he'd have to purchase an extension buckle for his plane seat.

"Thought you'd like it." His dad set the cake pan on the table.

"How about love?" Zax drew a knife through the steamy corn bread, and cut pieces big enough for a farmer-sized appetite. He served slices to his parents before plating one for himself. After prayer, he added thick pats of butter to his cake and took a bite. This had to be another heavenly delicacy.

"Good?" His mom always seemed to need the affirmation.

"Better." He took another bite. Yep, much better than good.

She beamed.

"What's on your agenda today?" Dad stuck a napkin between his shirt collar and neck, otherwise he always ended up with food on his work shirt.

"I took some pictures of a sunset last night. I think Corey was helping out God again. If any turn out, I have to do some work on them. Maybe add more artwork to the CorZa account."

"That's been going well?" His mom gently dabbed a napkin to the corners of her mouth.

"Very well. Corey's girls will have a nice little college fund awaiting them if it keeps building at this rate." Corey's artwork had sold well while he was alive, and had picked up even more since his death, so his daughters wouldn't have financial need. Even so, Zax preferred to give any of his CorZa—his photography business that he named for Corey and himself—profits to his nieces.

"It's a good thing you're doing, but maybe you should set aside funds for your own child as well."

Zax spit out his Johnny cake, having locked Gina's proposal and pregnancy in a back cabinet in his mind. "I, uh . . ." He wiped his mouth. "Uh, yeah, I suppose I should do that, too."

And maybe he should. True, he didn't have any legal or even any moral responsibility for the child, but being a single parent was tough enough without having to worry about paying for college. It wouldn't hurt him to start a savings account for Gina's little boy.

"Still getting used to the idea of being a father, huh?" His dad stuffed the last of his cake into his mouth.

"You could say that."

"Well, with as many jumpstarts as you and Corbin gave us, I've had no greater joy than raising you boys. Know that being a father isn't easy, but it's worth it."

Zax gulped. "Yeah, I'll keep that in mind." He hurried and finished his breakfast so he could get away from this conversation. Keeping Gina's secret was going to be tougher than he'd imagined. He excused himself from the table and put his dirty dishes in the dishwasher. "I'm going into town to do some work at the coffee shop."

"Will we see you for supper?" His mom kissed his cheek.

"Try keeping me away."

"Even if it's just pizza?"

"Especially if it's pizza." Even if it came from a chain. He'd missed the States' version of pizza over the last year. Or better yet, "How about if I pick some up from It's a Pastability on my way home?"

"Ah, now you're talking my language. I get a night off." Mom rubbed her hands together.

"As you should. I'll be home about five thirty." He ran upstairs to gather what he needed for work, then drove into town. He found an open parking space on the main drag and headed for the coffee shop. Why no one ever thought to open a beverage shop that offered something other than tea or coffee, he didn't know. And the coffee shops that served hot cocoa usually offered only three flavors: dark, milk, and white. Boring. Personally, he could drink different flavors of hot cocoa all year round.

But for now, the local coffee hangout, You've Been Served, opened by an attorney friend of Jon's who'd tired of the legal world, would have to do. He aimed for the shop, passing by some children's store, and he jerked to a stop. In the window display was a wood cradle with slatted sides and a rocker at its base.

Did Gina have something like that yet?

He detoured into the store and checked out the display up close.

"The rockers can be exchanged for rolling casters," a woman's voice said behind him.

Zax grinned, envisioning himself as a busy child, probably pushing the cradle all around the house. "Sounds dangerous."

"Only if you forget to lock the casters."

"Until kids figure out how to unlock them."

"By then, they've outgrown the cradle."

"Touché." He licked his finger and drew a number one

in the air. "That's one for you. My next question is, how much do you want for this?"

She named a figure that made his eyes pop wide open.

"How long will the child use this?" For that amount, it should eventually convert into an adult-sized bed.

"Three to four months is common. Depending upon the child, some use it up to six months."

"Hmm." Uh, no. He and his dad could make something like this for a tenth of the price. Would probably last longer, too. "Well, thanks for the info."

"It is handcrafted. You're not only getting a usable piece of furniture, but also a work of art. Perhaps your child could use it for a doll crib."

"Not my—" He stopped his sentence, not wanting to give up Gina's secret, even to a stranger. "I'll keep that in mind. Thank you."

He snapped a quick picture of the cradle then escaped from the baby store, feeling a sheen of sweat on the back of his neck, even in the cold temps. What had possessed him to enter in the first place? A crib? Why was he concerned about that?

He hurried toward the old bar-turned-coffee-shop, filing his impulsive decision into his brain's garbage file. He entered and spotted just the place he needed to concentrate on his project. After claiming the high-backed booth, he ordered a slice of lemon-poppyseed bread and a zebra hot cocoa—half dark chocolate, half white—with a dash of peppermint and a whole bunch of whipped cream on top.

Well, his mom always said he was high maintenance.

A minute or so later, his name was called, and he settled into his booth with his cocoa. He opened his Mac and sipped at his too-hot drink while sifting through the photographs he'd taken last night. They'd turned out far better than he'd hoped. Color exploded from his screen. Zax had no doubt that his little brother was Jesus's painting apprentice last night. His brother had loved color, and his paintings showed it.

These pictures should sell well as is, but Zax would also use a new program that helped turn photographs into watercolor or acrylic works of art. He was still experimenting with the program, figuring out to make it work the best for his purposes, but the pieces he'd put on his website had brought in more money than his regular photos. Even so, he preferred the unedited version. God's handiwork couldn't be improved upon.

"You busy?"

Zax startled and looked up at Jon, who sat opposite him in the booth, all dressed up for work with his button-down shirt and trademark bowtie.

"Working on adding to the CorZa gallery." He turned around his laptop. "Caught this sunrise on my way home last night."

"Wow," was all Jon said as he flipped through the shots. *Wow* was all that was needed. "Michaela will want to see these."

"Michaela?" His niece had hated her name since her dad moved in with his new family. "What happened to Six?

Mik?"

"That's the younger, less mature Michaela." Jon shook his head. "Next week, I expect something different. What am I getting into, marrying into a ready-made, mixed-up family? Should I run away?"

"Ah, you forget, Erin's a saint." He turned his Mac back around.

"Pretty much. Though she'd argue that point."

"Which, Mister Attorney, you probably thoroughly enjoy."

His friend grinned. "She does like to argue, but I usually win."

"Uh-uh. That's not how marriage works. Dad'll tell you the key is to always say, 'Yes, dear.'"

"Is that what you plan to do with Gina?"

Ah, the counselor deftly swoops in and drives home his main point of showing up here. The man had been wise to go into the legal profession. He never lost an argument. "What do you know?"

Jon spread open his hands open as if laying out all his cards. "I know that the baby isn't yours, and that the father has rescinded all parental rights. She told you that much?"

"Well, biology told me the child isn't mine. It's impossible."

"Really?"

"Why is that so hard to believe?"

"It's called a reputation."

"It's called boasting and a whole bunch of insinuation. I'm not the cad you think I am—was." Though he certainly wasn't lily-white either.

"I'm sorry." Jon raised his hands. "I tend to see the worst in people."

"As a divorce attorney, I'm sure you literally see the worst."

"True." He leaned back in the booth. "The proposal to Gina. Is it real? I couldn't tell. The look on your face last night said she ambushed you with the baby and the ring. But you didn't refute her, either. The Zax I know would have immediately denied her claims, if they were false."

Zax sighed and lifted a quick prayer, asking if he could tell Jon Gina's story. But his gut still told him to keep the pinky-swear promise he'd made to her, so he didn't respond at all.

"You and Gina are getting married." Jon's head seemed to be on a continuous swivel.

"That's what she says." Zax took a long swig of his drink, avoiding Jon's attorney gaze that likely made witnesses crack.

"I see." He drummed his fingers on the table. "Then let me give you one piece of advice. Don't hurt her. She's already been hurt enough, and you tend to be blind to the messes you leave behind."

Seriously? He slammed his drink glass on the table and hot cocoa sloshed onto his computer. Yeah, he'd made a lot of mistakes, but he wasn't a complete jerk. "Don't you have any criminals you need to put in jail?" Immediately, he lifted a silent apology for his burst of anger as he wiped the cocoa from his laptop. He was trying to do better, honestly he was, but people—make that friends—really made it difficult at times.

"I get the message." Jon stood and threw a couple of dollar bills onto the table. "Maybe you and I need to have it out on the racquetball court sometime."

"Only if you'd like me to wipe the floor with you."

"Big talk from someone who hasn't played me before."

"Big talk from someone who's always whooped you at sports." Though Zax had never played racquetball, he tended to catch on easily to athletic activities. "I'll take you up on the offer when I come up next week. What's good for you?"

Jon took out his phone and scrolled. "How about Friday night? Erin, your mom, and the girls have some wedding planning thing going on that I want to stay far away from."

"Perfect. That'll allow me more time to get stuff done back home." He recorded the date in his online calendar. "Oh, and loser supplies the Belden supper on the following Sunday."

"Winner gets to decide what that supper's going to be."

"You're on. I can taste that prime rib now."

"I was thinking a filet mignon or New York strip."

Zax waved toward the door. "Get outta here."

"See you next Friday, and be prepared to eat my dust."

Zax grinned, watching his friend leave. He liked that he and Jon could have differences, but that never stood in the way of their friendship.

This thing with Gina, though, seemed to be standing in

the way of a lot. He folded up his laptop and stuck it in his briefcase. What he needed to do was go back to the cities, where family and friends wouldn't dog him about Gina.

But first, she'd said they should get together to talk things over before he left town. He couldn't think of a better time than tomorrow night, if she wasn't busy. Dinner at Bear Tracks Bar & Grill would be good and wouldn't get her hopes up for anything romantic. Hopefully, she'd give him the okay to tell everyone the truth.

Chapter Four

"Don't wait up for me." Zax kissed his mom on the cheek and grabbed his winter coat from the closet. "Gina and I need to talk some things over tonight, and I don't know when I'll be home."

"Take all the time you need, but call if you're going to be home later than midnight. I don't want to worry. And drive carefully. It's slippery out there."

"Yeah, yeah, yeah. I get it." Still, he grinned. "Love you, Mom." He went out the front door and gingerly made his way down the snow-coated steps. A few years back, the mothering would have irritated him, now he realized it was a message of love.

After a day that had dumped five inches of snow, the flakes now floated lightly like a snow globe settling down. No doubt, the roads would be slick, so he'd take his mother's message to heart. He took his time on the less-traveled county roads, but when he reached the state highway, the road was mostly clear of ice and snow. In just a few minutes, he reached Gina's townhome.

He rang the doorbell and waited. Seconds later, she answered and stole his breath. He'd never thought pregnant women looked hot before, but Gina? That was the best word to describe her. She'd clearly spent time on her makeup and hair, but it was her outfit that turned him speechless. She wore a black, silky top that clung to her curves, including the baby bump. It was lacy around the neckline, showing just enough skin to be attractive without being revealing. Honestly, that was sexier than showing a lot of cleavage. Her top ended at her thighs that were covered with skinny jeans. And those high-heeled shoes she wore looked dangerous for someone who was pregnant, especially with this snow.

"Earth to Zax." She waved a hand in front of his eyes and grinned. "Made you look."

"Yeah." He scratched the back of his neck as he gazed beyond her. Anywhere but at her. "You about ready?" He stepped inside and shut the door, keeping the snow outdoors.

"I am more than ready." She opened her entry closet and took out a long coat and her purse. "It's been forever since I've gone dancing."

"Dancing?" He intentionally hadn't said anything about dancing, and chose a venue that didn't have it. At least it didn't use to.

"You didn't know? Bear Tracks added a dance floor a few months back. I've heard it's a hit. They feature local bands, but I haven't had anyone to go with. Guys take one look at me now, and well . . ." She smiled, but hurt shown in her eyes.

He couldn't add to that. "Then those guys have no taste. You look amazing."

"You're not just saying that?"

"Sweetheart, you saw my reaction when you opened the door."

She smiled genuinely this time. "I guess I did."

He assisted her with putting on her coat, while pondering his words. Was "sweetheart" an appropriate word to use for someone who was called to be a single missionary? More so, what about taking Gina out tonight? Was that appropriate? He had no plans beyond tonight. No plans even for dancing. Did those details matter? He'd have to take that up with his Boss during prayer. There was so much he needed to learn.

In the meantime, though, he planned to have a nice evening with Gina. They'd talk, he'd get her permission to tell the truth, and that would be it. Then he could move on with God's plans.

He escorted her to his car, and from there it took thirty minutes to reach the bar. They chose a booth near the back, furthest away from the band, so they could hear conversation better. Live music hadn't begun yet. Hopefully, they'd be long gone before the band started to warm up. Not that he didn't like dancing, but in his past, dancing at a bar too often led to another kind of dance he'd sworn off. And as sexy as she looked tonight, he'd be lying if he said it hadn't crossed his mind. God sure had some work to do with him yet!

Instead of looking at her, he shot his gaze around the filled room. Even here, Christmas lights twinkled, and paper mâché snowflakes hung from the ceiling. He loved how Christmas was celebrated in the States, even for those who didn't believe. Someday the veil would be lifted from others' eyes as well and they too would believe.

When the server arrived, he ordered a steak.

As did Gina.

He loved that she wasn't a dainty eater.

He talked about fishing with his dad the night before and catching their limit of sunfish. She mentioned how she'd love for her son to have a fishing partner someday. His dad certainly wouldn't mind. They laughed about his rideshare driver ditching him, and the Paul Bunyan lookalike who picked him up. They shed tears when talking about the deaths of Zax's brother and his wife. Gina had gotten to know both before the car accident.

Just like the other times they'd gotten together, the time was easily filled and seemed to zoom past. His plans to have dinner and head home were long forgotten. Yes, Gina had made bad choices with her ex-boyfriend, but who didn't make mistakes? He'd made plenty and many of them were doozies.

Gina was attractive, very attractive, but she was much more than that. She was funny and caring and smart. Far more intelligent than he was.

After the server cleared their dinner plates, they

ordered dessert. Gina told him she planned to continue her education and eventually take the bar, so she could be a partner to Jon instead of his assistant.

"But what about the baby?" blurted from his mouth without giving his brain time to stop him.

Her fork hovered in the air as if ready to skewer him. "Are you insinuating that mothers shouldn't go to school?"

"No." He squirmed in his seat and nibbled on his brownie.

Her grip tightened on that fork. "That I can't raise this child, work, and learn?"

He gulped, and finally his brain caught up to his mouth. "You can do anything, be anything you want, but you don't have to be a superhero. Yes, you are more than capable of doing it alone, but you don't have to."

"Which is exactly why I made that rash announcement two days ago. I know I can do it. And I know I'll be a fierce mama bear around this child, but I want better for him. I can do it alone, but I don't want to. A mom is good, but a mom and dad are better."

"Gina, I—"

She put a finger to his lips. "No. I shouldn't have cornered you like that, especially around your family. That was pregnancy hormones gone haywire. Let's just enjoy tonight. Someday down the road, if God wants my child to have a father, I have to trust that He'll provide."

"Very true. He will. Wait. You're a believer?"

She'd never mentioned any kind of faith before.

"When your poor life decisions suddenly leave you

pregnant and single, you start listening to your boss. I'd always pooh-poohed Jon's faith, but when he stood up for me, helped me get what's-his-face out of my life for good, without judging me one time, yeah, I listened. Finally."

"Huh. Well, you'll never guess what happened to me in Israel." And he told the story he'd shared with his parents the other day. Oh, he loved telling the story, ending with his baptism in the Jordan River.

"That must have been amazing."

"It was . . ." He searched for the right words, but nothing came. "Indescribable. To be baptized where John baptized Jesus? It was overwhelming. I must have cried for an hour."

"You're a softy."

He shrugged. "Don't let the word get out."

"I promise." She smiled.

And his stomach did that topsy-turvy thing it did when he was very attracted to someone. Lord, help him.

A band finished their warm-ups and began playing "I'll Be Home for Christmas." Zax's appendages suddenly had minds of their own. He stood and offered his hand. "Care to dance?"

She laid her hand in his and stood. "I didn't think you were going to ask."

"I didn't think so either." Dancing was okay for a missionary, wasn't it? After all, there was dancing in the Bible. King David danced, too.

As long as that was all they did, Zax didn't see a problem. So, he led her to the dance floor and then pressed his open hand behind her back and held her loosely. He couldn't help but breathe in. Was that peppermint?

She hummed along to the music as they swayed.

That song ended, and they danced to "White Christmas" then "Jingle Bell Rock" and "Bless the Broken Road." That one wasn't a Christmas tune, but it fit his life. Gina's life. And like at his baptism in the Jordan River, tears slipped over his cheeks.

He knew one thing at this moment.

He had to leave. Now. Because somehow, he was falling for Gina Holmquist, and the only thing that could come of that was two broken hearts.

Chapter Five

After dropping Gina off, Zax hurried back to his parents' home, hoping his mom hadn't stayed up. He'd been so distracted by his date that he'd forgotten to call and let his mom know he'd be home after midnight.

He hadn't planned to be out that late. Hadn't even realized what time it was until the band played their last number. He was in trouble, deep trouble, and not just with his mom. This Christmas was one big mess.

The lights were on in the front room of his folks' home. Not a surprise as they'd always left them on until he and or Corey arrived home safely. Usually, a parent remained up as well. Hopefully, at thirty-plus years old, he'd grown past that stage.

He parked in the driveway then entered through a side door and stored his winter gear in a closet. All was silent. So far, so good. He walked through the kitchen and down the hallway toward the stairs.

"Trying to sneak past?"

Dad.

He turned toward the family room where his dad sat in the recliner, with a book in his hand.

"Was worth a try."

"Let's have a chat."

In years past, that meant, "Let me tell you what your punishment is for arriving home so late."

Curious, Zax plopped down on the couch. "What's up? Besides you, of course." He laughed at his stupid joke.

Dad just shook his head. "I've been thinking." He removed his glasses, wiped his eyes, then put his glasses back on. "This whole engagement seems off."

Zax scrubbed at a dirty spot on his jeans. "How so?"

"Gut feeling."

"Your gut isn't always right."

"It's more right than wrong."

"True." Gina had given him permission to tell the truth, and this was the perfect opportunity, but words failed him. Instead, changing the subject, he took out his phone and brought up the picture of the cradle. "I have a question for you."

He showed the pic to his dad. "Could you and I make this?"

Dad stared at the picture, then up at Zax with an expression Zax couldn't interpret.

That irritated him. This was how Erin must feel when she struggled with reading body language.

With the phone in hand, his dad stood. "Let me show

you something."

Zax followed his dad upstairs and into an unfinished space used for storage. Dad flicked on the light, then walked to something covered in a sheet, which he removed.

A cradle. Very similar to the one he'd seen in the store. But better.

Zax knelt and studied the workmanship, running his hand over the smooth cherry surface. "When did you do this?"

"It was Clara's. Your brother brought me a similar picture when Lilith was expecting. I was still working at forgiving him for walking out on Erin and Michaela. Crafting this together helped mend our rift. When he and Lilith died, Jon made sure the cradle got back to me."

Zax looked up at his dad. "Could Gina use it?"

"Just Gina?"

"The baby, I mean." Zax felt as if he was digging a hole too deep to climb out of.

"*The* baby." Dad crossed his arms. "Seems to me that if you're going to be doing mission work, this would be rather cumbersome to drag around."

Yep, definitely digging a hole. He couldn't respond directly to his dad's statement, so he brought the subject back to the beginning. "Can she use it?"

"I think that would please your mother."

But not his father, apparently.

"Thank you." He stood and realized he could now look down on his father. Still, Zax would always look up to the man and coveted his approval. "I'm heading to the cities tomorrow morning, but I'll be back in town next week. Thursday night maybe. I could bring it to her then."

"I'll have it all polished up for you."

"You don't have to—"

"Yes, son, yes I do."

"Of course." Zax needed to get out of this attic, away from the cradle and this conversation. He felt as if he was being dishonest with his father.

And to himself.

Tonight had done a number on him.

He led the way out of the storage room and stopped by his bedroom door. "Thanks, Dad. For everything."

"You know I'd do anything for you."

"Yeah, I do." He stuck his hands in his pockets, trying to think of something to lighten the conversation, and he knew just what to bring up. He grinned and looked directly at his father. "Apparently all the women are doing wedding stuff next Friday, so Jon and I are going to have it out on the racquetball court. You up to watching me beat the stuffing out of him?"

Dad laughed. "From what I hear about Jon's skills, you might be eating those words. But yeah, I'd like that."

Yeah. Zax would too.

Notebook in hand, Zax sat in his recliner, taking notes on his finished—but in need of tweaking—story, watching it play out on his fifty-inch screen. Over the past week and a half, he'd worked eighteen-hour days on his *Walking Through the New Testament* piece. Just watching it overwhelmed his heart.

Before he'd gone on this assignment, he'd always believed that the Old Testament and New Testament were about completely different Gods, but now he knew without a doubt that both testaments were intricately linked like strands of DNA. One wasn't complete without the other. Maybe he should do a piece on *Walking Through the Old Testament*, followed by *Bible DNA*. Okay, that last title was hokey, though the concept sounded interesting.

But he could no longer tell those stories through secular eyes.

He couldn't even finish *this* project without injecting his Christian bias. It was impossible. Would his employers see that and reject his piece?

Didn't matter if they did. He'd remind them that telling the truth and being fair and accurate, were part of The Journalist's Creed written by Walter Williams a century ago. Even that claimed that "the journalism that succeeds best . . . fears God and honors man."

Zax wouldn't change a thing, especially his testimony at the end of the piece, showing his baptism. That was what walking with Jesus did.

Once complete, the documentary would last around twelve hours. His employers would be airing it on public TV sometime next year over a six-day period. Probably during Holy Week.

He hit the remote, turning off the TV, and smiled. Very satisfied.

His family would be proud.

He was proud of this piece, probably the best work he'd ever done. He couldn't wait to do more.

But what about the mission trip God called him to.

What about Gina?

He closed his eyes and slumped in the chair. What about Gina?

He'd talked with her every day, telling her about his story. They laughed about Jon suddenly becoming scatterbrained because the only thing he could focus on was his upcoming marriage. The guy was completely in love. Had been for years.

Then Gina would complain about a couple who wanted a divorce because they didn't love each other anymore and how she and Jon wanted to bash their heads together and remind them love was a verb. It required action.

Action.

He blew out his breath and decided to take a walk to the Mississippi. See if he could hear God any better down there. Somehow, being back in the States, God's voice had lost its clarity, and Zax needed to fix that. Here, he had so many distractions. Gina. Work. His parents. Gina. Jon and Erin's wedding. Christmas shopping. Gina.

Yeah, it all came back to her. Tomorrow night he was seeing her, bringing over the cradle fashioned by his dad and brother. Why? What did that say about his feelings for her?

He dressed for the ten-degree weather and headed outside. The river was about five blocks away, a good brisk walk. There was nothing like cold air to clear his senses, to empty his mind of Gina.

She was easily the biggest distraction. That meant, the sooner he left Minnesota for the mission field, the better. And after that two-year commitment was over, then he'd finance the Old Testament story on his own.

The apostle Paul remained single. Zax could too. All he had to do was put the focus right where it needed to be. On Jesus.

He reached the river and found a snow-covered bench overlooking the water. He sat, closed his eyes, and took in the crackle of the icy water, wind hurrying through leafless trees, traffic crunching over the snow-covered road behind him.

Then, like he did overseas, he pictured Jesus hurrying to sit alongside him. Zax spoke his thoughts out loud, not caring if joggers along the path thought he was whacky.

"Thanks, Jesus, for meeting me here today."

"I'm always here for you," he imagined Jesus saying as He handed Zax a mug of hot cocoa topped with whipped cream. "Tell me what's going on."

Then Zax spilled out from his heart. His belief that he was called into missions. Gina's surprise. His unwanted, growing feelings toward her. They barely knew each other, but when they got together, it felt as if they'd known each other forever. Before coming home, nothing had been further from his mind than marriage and children. And now suddenly, that was what he pictured at night before going to sleep? What was wrong with him? Never before had he desired settling down. Why now when he and God had other plans?

He imagined Jesus asking, "Have you looked for answers in the scriptures?"

Sure. He read the Bible every day.

But, did he listen for answers when reading?

He pulled out his phone and removed a glove to scroll through the scriptures. Where should he even begin?

Christmas was only two weeks away, so that was where he'd start. He turned to Luke then Matthew. He read through chapter one, then reread verses eighteen through twenty-five talking about Joseph. His betrothed was pregnant, and not with his child. Back then, that was a serious offense for the woman, and the punishment could mean death. Yet, after the angel implored Joseph not to fear, he stayed with Mary and became Jesus's father.

Was fear Zax's issue? Afraid his past sins would disqualify him from being a good father? Afraid he'd make the same adulterous choice as his younger brother? Afraid to give up the control singleness brought him? Maybe he was afraid he was hearing God wrong, and that in choosing missions over marriage he was making an erroneous choice. Or vice versa.

Zax continued to pray for clarity as he read and reread Matthew one. By the time he went to bed that evening, he knew exactly what he needed to do.

Zax lugged the cradle up the steps to Gina's door, set it down, and rang the doorbell. She was expecting him for their date, another evening at Bear Tracks, but she wouldn't anticipate this gift. He couldn't wait to see her expression when she saw it.

The door flung upon and she smiled. Dazzling.

"Surprise!" He motioned to the crib, and her smile faded slow as a sunset.

She wasn't happy?

"For me?"

"What do you think of it? My dad made it."

"I . . ." She shook her head, but didn't smile. "Bring it on in."

He grunted as he lifted it and carried it over the threshold, then set it down in the entry so he could remove his boots. "Where do you want it?"

"Um . . ." She looked toward a set of stairs leading up, then motioned straight ahead. "Living room's good for now."

"I can bring it to the nursery."

"Zax, it's a nice gift and all, but . . ."

"But what? You have one already?"

"No, that's not it." She sighed. "I can't accept such a special gift from you. This needs to stay in your family."

He allowed a half grin and put his hands on her hips, drawing her close. This wasn't how he'd planned the evening to go, but he was all for spontaneity. "What if you're part of my family?"

"Zax . . ." She pushed away and hugged herself, clearly fighting back tears. "This is"—she looked to the ceiling and shook her head—"undoubtedly the sweetest thing anyone's ever done for me, but I can't do that to you. I know I initiated the idea, but that was whacky pregnancy hormones. I told you, I'm going to be fine. I've got a good job. The best boss. I don't need you."

That sentence hit him in the gut, and he stepped back. No, she was just saying that to let him off the hook. "I know you don't need me, and that's what I love about you." He rested a hand on her cheek.

She pushed his hand away and laughed. "Love, Zax? What do you know about love? Love is more than sex. It's waking up beside me when I have no makeup on. It's thinking I'm beautiful even after I've had a baby and have stretch marks all over my belly. It's keeping house and changing diapers and budgeting. It's growing old, gray, and fat together, and that's not who you are."

"How do you know? Maybe that's exactly who I am." He wanted to take her in his arms, hold her, convince her she was wrong, so he rammed his hands into his pockets. "Tell me you don't love me."

"You're sweet, Zachary Belden, and so much fun to be around." She pressed a hand to his cheek and looked to the ceiling, then back at him. Noticeable tears clung to her cheeks. "But sweet and fun doesn't equate to love."

"You don't love me?"

"I barely know you. We've had fun, but that doesn't

make for a lasting marriage, like your parents'. I see too much divorce in my job every day, and I will not do that to my son."

"I've seen what divorce does, too. Close up. I won't allow that to happen to us."

"You're right. You won't, because we're not getting married. Maybe it's best if we don't see each other anymore so these stray feelings don't get in the way again."

"Stray feelings?" He blinked. "Just like that, we're done?"

"We were never a 'we' in the first place."

"I see." He clenched his jaw, holding back his own tears. How stupid he'd been. How blind he was to think he'd heard from God last night. Made him want to take his Bible and rip it apart. "Fine then. Keep the cradle. I won't ever have use for it."

He stepped into his boots and stomped from the townhouse, then slammed the door shut behind him. He slammed the door on his car, too. He was a fool. If he'd heard God wrong in this, how did he know that he'd been right about anything? Maybe he wasn't called to be a missionary either.

He zoomed away from her complex. Maybe he'd gotten so caught up in his emotions that he'd forgotten how to think like a rational human being. That was what had happened to his brother, who got so caught up in his feelings for Lilith that he walked away from his marriage and daughter. Stupid.

Zax had vowed not to be like his brother. Guess he'd

failed in that, too.

Driving through town, the neon lights of a liquor store grabbed his attention and lured him into the parking lot, then into the building. It had been a while since he'd had a whiskey straight. It had been a long time since he'd been this teed off.

Once back in the car, he squealed from the parking lot and aimed for his folks' place. Minutes later, he pulled into their driveway. Too few minutes, which meant he'd been going way over the speed limit and was lucky he hadn't been pulled over by a cop or landed in a ditch. Yeah, emotions made him stupid. Times like this, he envied Erin's gift for deep feeling and her pragmatism.

He stalked into the house, right past his parents, who were having supper. He hurried to his bedroom and made a call to the company he'd signed on with for the next two years. Voice mail picked up, no surprise, but that was just fine. He'd rather leave a message than speak with an actual person right now. "This is Zachary Belden. I've changed my mind about taking a position with you. Thank you for the offer." Then he hung up. At least he'd been polite.

He opened his bottle of whiskey and took a healthy slug, liking the way it burned down his throat. A few more long chugs, and he was feeling much better.

Maybe he could make that next story about *Walking Through the Old Testament* from a secular perspective after all.

Chapter Six

Zax awoke swearing a car had hit him last night. Every bone, muscle, tendon, and cell in his body ached, and a hammer still pounded in his head. Along with having cotton mouth, his throat burned from all his trips to the bathroom last night.

What had he done?

Pound. Pound. Pound. Came at his bedroom door and echoed in his head.

"You up?" Dad. Naturally.

"Yeah," barely screeched from his mouth. He cleared his throat. "Not feeling well."

The door opened, like he was still a child who needed to be checked on. His dad walked in with a tray holding a bottle of water, aspirin, a banana, dry toast, and bacon.

Bacon?

He set the tray at the foot of Zax's bed. "Heard all your trips to the john last night." He bent and picked up the empty whiskey bottle from the floor and clutched it in his hand.

Zax grunted. Of course, they'd heard him. They were parents, and parents were gifted with radar and supersensitive hearing to know whenever their kids messed up.

It was a good thing Gina had turned him down last night. No doubt, that radar-vision hadn't been gifted to him. He'd stink as a parent. All he did when things went wrong was drink it away or spend the evening with a beautiful woman. He was a class A jerk. Gina was right. She didn't need him. She deserved much better.

"Jon's expecting you in a couple hours, you—"

"What?" Zax jerked toward the clock—"Ouch!"—and regretted doing that. It couldn't be three in the afternoon. And what was his dad doing home? "You take the day off to babysit?"

"Decided to work from home."

Zax laid back down. Maybe he could sleep away the aches. No way could he survive a game of racquetball. "Tell Jon I'm sick."

"You have a phone. Tell him yourself."

"Fine." He grabbed his phone from the bed stand and scrolled to Jon's name.

"But then you treat the family to New York strip on Sunday."

Grrrr. He forgot about that. He hated losing. Especially this way.

"Fine. I'll play." He'd worked through a hangover many

times before. He could do it again. He downed the aspirin and water then threw off his covers and realized he was still dressed in his jeans from last night.

"Want to talk about it?"

Zax cursed.

His dad didn't even flinch. "Guess not." Dad bent over, picked up something, and threw it onto the bed. Then he walked to the door and stopped. "But know I'm here whenever you're ready."

"Yeah. I know. Thanks." Even those few words hurt his brain. How was he ever going to challenge Jon?

He laid back down and something nicked him in the shoulder. He reached over to brush whatever it was away. A book?

He picked it up, planning to lay it on his bed stand, but then he realized what book it was.

His Bible.

"Nice try, Dad." He hurled the book across the room, and it whooshed into his garbage can. "Nothing but net. Bring it on, Jon."

Problem was, Zax had never played racquetball before and knew nothing about it. On his phone, he brought up a video and studied the game while downing the food his dad had brought up. He'd be ready for the match if it killed him.

Zax stepped into the rectangular room onto a wood floor

with random red lines drawn across it. The racket felt small and foreign in his gloved hand. He'd thought it would feel more like a tennis racket than it did. And for some reason, he'd expected the ball to be fuzzy, not rubber.

Oh, this was going to be a first-class drubbing, and Jon would rightfully rub Zax's nose in it.

Jon slapped him on the back, and Zax wheezed trying to hold in the pain.

"Ready?" Jon bounced the ball on the court.

"How about we warm up first, let me get a feel for the court."

"Sure thing." Jon bounced the ball and hit it toward the wall in front of him. It ricocheted off of it and toward Zax.

He flailed at the ball and wound up face down on the floor.

A moan came from behind him where his dad sat as the lone spectator. He was probably enjoying this immensely.

Jon gave him a hand up. "Your reactions were a bit slow. Let's try it again." Jon bounced the ball then hit it off the wall.

Zax raced toward it. Swung. Missed. Cursed.

"Language." His dad yelled out.

Zax flexed his muscles and stood back, balancing on the balls of his feet. "Bring it."

The ball banged off the wall, and sailed right for Zax's head. He dove to the floor, but it still nicked off the side of his head.

He held his head in his hands. "Fine. I give. You win. Steak's on me."

"I think the mis-stakes on you. Gina called in sick today." Jon offered his hand.

Zax slapped it away.

"She never calls in sick." Jon hovered over Zax, a storm cloud brewing on his face.

"Then obviously there's some bug going around." Zax pulled himself into a standing position and slowly stood. How had he ever thought he was going to play a game of racquetball? What an idiot.

"Yeah, I'm pretty sure I know what that bug is." Jon let Zax dad know they'd be back shortly, then led Zax off the court into an otherwise empty locker room.

Zax slumped on a bench.

And Jon hovered over him, staring him down as if he were a good-for-nothing criminal. "How much did you drink last night?"

"None o' your business." Zax returned the glare.

"It won't make the pain go away."

Zax gritted his teeth. "What pain?"

Jon's eyes softened. "Nothing hurts more than a broken heart."

"Aren't you the funny guy?" Zax pulled off his shirt as he thought of a comeback to deflect from himself. "I saw Gina last night and know for a fact she has no reason to have a broken heart."

"No reason?" Jon shook his head and took a seat across from Zax. "Let me lay out the facts to you." He held up one finger. "She announces your engagement, and you comply."

"What choice did I have?"

Jon held up another finger. "You go on a date and wind up closing down the place."

"It's what I do. I like to show my dates a good time." He smirked and wagged his brows. "If you know what I mean."

"Has anyone ever told you alcohol makes you a jerk?"

"Not true. I'm the life of the party when I drink. It's the hangover that makes me a buzzkill."

Jon leaped up and slammed his fist into the locker right behind Zax.

"Whoa." Zax squeezed his fingers into his palms, trying to ward away the reverberation in his brain.

"Grow up, Zax." Jon massaged his hand. "Here I thought Gina had been stupid for turning you down. Guess we know—"

"Wait. How do you know she turned me down?" Zax leaped up and went nose to nose with his friend. "You weren't there last night."

Jon shoved him away. "No, but Erin went over there today to pick up the pieces."

"What pieces? She's the one who broke my heart, not the other way around."

Jon grinned, and Zax wanted to smack that stupid grin from his face.

"You just proved my point." Jon held up a third finger. "You, my friend, are suffering from a broken heart."

Zax opened his mouth, but nothing came out. The lawyer had cleverly coaxed out a confession Zax hadn't wanted to admit to himself. He plopped down on the bench and held his head in his hands. "I don't know how it happened. I didn't intend to fall for her. Didn't want to. My life was planned out. I thought God was calling me to the mission field. And now . . . now I don't know if I've been hearing God right."

"Oh, I think you were hearing Him fine, just the details got fuzzy."

"How so?"

"People forget that we're all missionaries right where God has planted us. In my job, I'm pointing people to Jesus whenever I can. Look at your parents and how their home is always open and welcoming. Even in their accounting business, their faith isn't hidden. And then there's Corey. Your brother's life testimony is living on through his artwork. Don't forget about the project you've been working on. If your walk through the New Testament had that kind of impact on you, just think how God will use it to influence others."

"You think so?"

"I know so."

"Well, I thought I knew a lot more than I do. Last night I read Matthew one over and over again about Joseph staying with Mary when he didn't have to, when the child wasn't his. I thought for sure that's what God wanted me to do. And Gina turned me down flat. What was I supposed to do?"

"Persistence, my friend." Jon laid a hand on Zax's shoulder then sat beside him. "Do you know how long I pined for Erin? Since we were kids. And then she and

Corey got together and divorced, and I kept thinking Corey was going to wake up and go back to her. It wasn't until he died that I made my move, and only because God kept nudging me. Even then it took way too long to convince her that she loved me back."

"Does that mean Gina will give me a second chance? Will God give me another chance? I mean, I threw my Bible into the garbage, man. I'm surprised I wasn't struck dead by a bolt of lightning. What was I thinking?"

"You were hurting. God gets it. And He's the Champion of forgiveness. Besides, I've never known you to give up so quickly. If I were a coach, I'd tell you to get your behind out there—"

"No coach would say 'behind.'"

"—and win one for the team."

Zax shook his head. "I'm living in an alternate reality. Mr. Nerd is giving me sports and romance advice."

"What can I say?" Jon rubbed his knuckles against his chest. "They don't call me the Romance Lawyer for nothing."

Zax snorted.

And Jon laughed. "It fit my spiel."

"Well, Mr. Romance Lawyer." Zax got up and nodded to the showers. "Guess I need to do some cleaning up if I'm going to do any romancing."

"Yeah. And don't forget your breath, dude. It's nasty. No woman's gonna kiss that."

"Truth. And if things go my way, I plan to do some heavy-duty kissing."

Chapter Seven

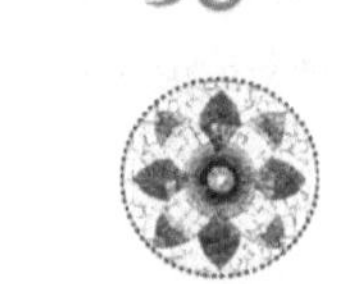

Zax pulled up in front of Gina's townhome entrance and took a deep breath. Shoot, he was nervous. You'd think he was a romance rookie the way his nerves zinged. The difference was, this time was for keeps.

He got out of his car and made sure his tie was straight and his suitcoat wasn't tucked into the back of his pants. From the backseat, he took a bouquet that had a sprig or two of mistletoe in it. Sure, it was corny, but she liked corny. And fun.

Taking another deep breath, he walked up her sidewalk, then released the breath. She was home, he knew that, as he'd enlisted Erin's help for the evening, making sure Gina was going to be there when he arrived. Tonight wasn't going to be about babies and cradles—maybe that was where he'd gone wrong. She wanted to be loved for her, not for the baby.

If she said no tonight, he'd be back tomorrow and the

next day and the next and let her know he wasn't going away.

He rang the doorbell and held the bouquet behind his back, listening.

Silence answered for what had to be a minute, so he pressed the bell again just as the door opened.

They both startled.

"Zax?" She stood there in a long T-shirt and jogging pants with her hair pulled back in a messy bun. Not a lick of makeup on her face.

Man, she was beautiful.

She crossed her arms over her chest as if wanting to hide her wardrobe. "What do you want?"

"I'd like to start over again." He handed her the bouquet. "Date you properly this time."

She blinked. "What?"

"Mind if I come in? It's drafty out here." Freezing, actually, but he didn't want to complain.

"Uh, I'm not really dressed for company."

He pulled off his tie, took off his jacket, and untucked his shirt. "There. Me neither."

"You're crazy."

"Jury's out."

She laughed, and man did that sound good.

"Fine. Come on in. But I don't have any food."

He checked his watch. "Pizza should be here in about thirty minutes."

"Pizza?"

"You like pizza, don't you? Because if you don't, that's sort of a deal breaker."

"I happen to love pizza." Finally, she made room for him to enter her small foyer.

The cradle had been moved to her living room, tucked in a corner, looking like it belonged here. She gestured to a chair across from her sofa where she sat, her legs crossed, the bouquet right beside her. At least she hadn't thrown it in the garbage.

"What are you doing here?" She fiddled with a blanket edge.

He sat on the edge of his seat and headed toward her. "I came to apologize."

"Dressed like that?"

"I wanted to give my best."

"Well, you did look pretty good."

"Not anymore?"

She grinned, tucking her chin. "You pull off this look pretty well, too."

"I do my best." His smile curved up to the right, then flattened. He tented his hands below his chin. "But seriously, I need to apologize. I came here last night, all cocky, thinking I was God's gift to you. Literally. That's what I took from the Bible, that I was doing you this big favor. That I was being all Joseph-like and rescuing you, when you didn't need to be rescued. I wasn't doing you any favors. I tend to forget, not everything's about me." He splayed open his hands, hoping to show he was open to hearing from her, hoping he'd learn to listen.

She uncrossed her legs, letting her feet settle on the floor, and she leaned toward him. "And I didn't want to be your charity wife. I want to marry someone because we love each other and promise to love—as in action—each other. I know it's all my fault for starting this. That night at your folks' place, I would have eloped. Since then, I've screwed my head on straight, thank goodness."

"Then I guess my important question for the night is, do you love me?" He held his breath, waiting for an answer.

But she looked to the ceiling, as if searching for a way out, then back at Zax. "That night four months ago, when you left here because you said you respected me too much to make love to me, I think I fell in love with you then."

Dare he hope?

"And when I went crying back to what's-his-face and we . . ." She blinked and looked away, wiping her eyes. "I realized what he and I had wasn't love or respect, but a lot of control. Jon had warned me about him, but did I listen?" She curved her hands beneath her baby. "So, when I watch your parents' relationship, Jon and Erin's, I want that for myself."

Zax got up and crossed the room, then squatted on the floor at Gina's feet. "I'm not my dad, and I'm certainly not Jon. I can only be me, and I'm a work in progress. When I came home a few weeks back, I was so excited about being like Paul and going on a mission trip, but I've learned—thanks to Jon kicking my butt at racquetball today—that I don't have to travel the world to be a missionary. God'll use me right here or wherever He directs. I'm not the apostle Paul. I'm Zachary Belden, messed-up child of God."

He reached for Gina's hand, and thankfully, she laid

hers in his.

"Gina, I can promise you that you will be cherished. I can promise that when I wake up beside you every day, I'll thank God for you. And I never want to hold you back. If you want to take the bar, I'll be cheering you on. I'll change diapers even if I have to pinch a clothespin over my nose, and when you grow old and gray and chubby, you'll still be the most beautiful woman in the world to me."

She giggled and shook her head. "You should really take back that last promise. I don't want you to lie."

"It's not a lie." He got up on his knees. "So, my question is, do you want to date me, or do you want to skip all that and go right to the marriage?"

She laughed out loud.

"Wow. That's one way to make a guy feel secure."

She cradled her hand beneath his chin and lifted.

Oh, man, her eyes were aimed right at his lips.

Hard as it was, he held back.

"I think dating's a good idea." She narrowed the distance between them, her gaze still on his lips. "And since we've already been on, what has it been, four or five dates?"

"About five." He couldn't resist inching closer to her.

"Hmm." She pulled back.

Oh, come on!

"Five is a good number, don't you think?" She lifted the bouquet and sniffed.

"Five is an excellent number." He shifted on the floor. His knees were getting tired and sore, but this moment was worth it.

She raised her left hand. The ring he'd seen on her ring finger had shifted to the middle. She held her hand toward him. "That's my grandma's engagement ring. I hope it's okay for you."

Instead of answering, he slipped the ring from her middle finger to the one beside it. "Does that mean you'll marry me?"

She picked up the bouquet and held it in the air above their heads. "I noticed you have some mistletoe in here."

"You know, my knees are getting really sore here."

"Then stand up so I can say yes properly."

It was about time.

He stood and wrapped both arms around her waist, pulled her close against him, and feathered his lips across hers, turning his stomach in knots. She deepened the kiss, and he moaned his appreciation as her hands wove through his hair.

Oh, man, he was a goner.

She pulled back slightly, her gaze meeting his. "Does that answer your question?"

"Mm, hmm." He tried kissing her again, but she held back and placed a finger at his lips.

"I have one request."

"Anything." And right now, he honestly would give her anything.

"I would like a very short engagement."

He grinned. "That I think I can manage."

And they sealed that promise with a kiss.

Epilogue

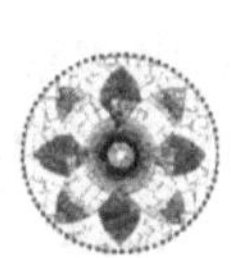

"Whose idea was it again to have a double wedding?" Zax looked in the mirror in Jon's master bath as he adjusted his tie. Just a regular tie, not a bowtie like Jon wore, but then that was what Jon always wore. It fit him.

"That would be our fiancées."

"Actually, that would be *your* fiancée."

Erin hated being the center of attention, and this was her second wedding, so she'd brought up the idea. Gina had immediately latched onto it and Zax and Jon had just stood back and nodded, "Yes, dear."

But now, this was the real thing. He, Zachary Belden, had gone from being a confirmed lifelong bachelor to engaged and about to be married in a matter of three-and-a-half weeks. And he was ecstatic. That was a miracle only God could pull off.

Someone knocked on the bathroom door and Zax's dad poked his head in. "Ready, guys?"

They looked at each other and grinned.

"Race you out." Jon bolted from the room, past Zax's dad.

And Zax chased after, elbowing past Jon in the hallway leading to the great room of Jon's A-frame home overlooking a lake. In the middle of the window was the tallest Christmas tree Zax had ever seen, and it was decorated with precision, clearly Erin's doing. Behind the pastor, the sun was just beginning to descend. Again, the timing was Erin's handiwork, no doubt. Too bad he couldn't whip out his camera and snag a few shots. Hopefully, the photographer Erin had hired would seize the opportunity.

A small handful of people sat in cushy chairs set up in rows in the center of the room. Zax and Jon took their places in front of the guests with Zax resisting the urge to elbow Jon. His mom, seated in the front row, shook her head at his antics. He just shrugged. That was what they got for asking two friends to share their wedding. Some roughhousing should be expected, right?

"Boys." The pastor whispered sharply and gestured for them to get into place beside an arrangement of poinsettias.

Friends and family giggled.

Didn't matter to him. All he really cared about was standing there until he said, "I do." Oh, and kissing the bride, of course.

And then the music started. "O Come, All Ye Faithful." A family friend played the viola, another the flute, and a third played piano.

He eyed the stairway that led down from the second floor. A lighted garland circled the banister. Clutching a single red rose in her hand, its stem wrapped in white, Clara hopped down from one step to the next, her blond ringlets bouncing along. Corey would have laughed out loud to see his exuberant daughter. Good thing Erin had vetoed a floor-length dress for the child. She'd have tumbled down the stairs. The red ribbon in her hair, that matched the dress, was already starting to fall out.

Michaela followed her half-sister, also holding a single rose. Actually, this week she was going by the nickname *Six* because her father had called her that. She loved Jon, but seeing her mom marry someone else still wasn't easy. Using Corey's nickname for her was one way of honoring and remembering him.

Corey would no doubt be very happy with that.

No surprise, Six broke with tradition, refusing to wear a dress, and donned a jumpsuit instead. Still, his teenage niece looked pretty sharp. Jon had his hands full with that one—boys were going to be knocking down the doors really soon.

She stopped midway down the flight and stared straight ahead, past him and Jon.

He turned and grinned. God's multicolored, ever-changing Christmas lights shown outside the window. Now that was a sunset worth photographing.

By the tears leaking from his niece's eyes, he knew she was thinking about her dad painting right alongside Jesus.

The music changed to a song called “Still, Still, Still,” something Erin had picked out. It fit her perfectly.

Zax looked back at the staircase, and his breath caught.

Wow! Erin stood at the top, her dark curls cascading over bare shoulders. She was a knockout. Zax stole a quick look at Jon, who was wiping his nose. The guy had turned into a big softy.

She slowly came down the stairs, her red, white, and green bouquet held in front. Her gaze riveted on Jon the entire way as she walked the short aisle to take his arm. Zax couldn’t be happier for a couple.

Well, except for him and Gina.

The music changed to “O Holy Night,” drawing his attention back to the top of the stairway. Gina stood there in a pinkish satiny dress, her blond hair curling around her head. Stealing his breath. He now understood what “knees buckling” meant. Holy cow, was she stunning. She seemed to float down the steps, holding her bouquet of pinkish flowers and trailing greens in front of her. It didn’t completely hide her baby bump but didn’t draw attention to it either. Was he a lucky man or what?

Wearing a big grin, she took her time walking up the aisle, clearly relishing all the attention. At last, she passed the final chair, and he stepped forward to take her arm. At that moment, the rest of the world became a haze. The pastor did some talking, read passages from the Bible, and did more talking. They said their “I wills” and exchanged their vows and rings, followed by more Christmas music while Erin, Jon, and the girls poured sand together, blending their family. He and Gina went the traditional route with a unity candle. More music.

And then the part he was waiting for.

The pastor said, "Jon and Erin, I now pronounce you husband and wife."

Zax heard a relieved sigh from Erin and suddenly she was tugging on Jon's hand to hurry down the aisle.

Jon managed to pull her back and whispered. "What about the kiss?"

"Geez, Mom," came from Six.

Erin's face was as red as her daughter's dress as she stood on her tiptoes to kiss her husband. A way-too-quick-kiss, in Zax's opinion. And just like that, the two were practically jogging down the aisle to boisterous clapping and cheering. The musicians could barely keep up with their rendition of "Ode to Joy." No doubt, Erin was very relieved that her part of the ceremony was over.

As soon as they reached the back, the attendees all turned to the front, so they didn't see Jon give Erin an edgy PG-13-rated kiss. Attaboy. Erin didn't seem to mind either.

"Get a room," Six said under her breath.

Zax just chuckled. He couldn't wait to hear her commentary on his and Gina's kiss, one they'd choreographed a few weeks back and spent many evenings rehearsing.

The pastor, grinning from having watched the newly married couple, now looked to Zax and Gina. He said some more words that went in and out of Zax's ears before he finally heard what he'd been waiting for. "Zachary and

Gina, by the authority vested in me by the State of Minnesota, I now pronounce you husband and wife." A smirk spread across his face. "You may kiss your bride." As if Zax would forget.

Not a chance.

"Don't mind if I do." He pulled Gina into his arms gave her a G-rated peck, like Erin had given Jon, but then, wagging his brows, Zax tugged a fan from his back pocket and handed it to Gina. With a flick of her wrist, the fan spread open, as she'd been practicing all week. She held it in front of their faces as he dipped her and gave her a proper wedding kiss.

"Seriously?" Six's commentary. Zax could envision her rolling her eyes. "You all need to get a room."

That was the plan, dear Michaela.

But first they needed to celebrate with family and friends.

The musical trio began playing Zax's choice, "Linus and Lucy," that jazzy piano song in *A Charlie Brown Christmas*.

He and Gina did a choreographed dance down the aisle, and then they shared a third, longer kiss.

And that was just the beginning.

He couldn't wait to spend a lifetime sharing kisses and dancing and messy adventures with her.

Read more about Zax and the Belden family in
A Beautiful Mess (The Mosaic Collection).

A Note from the Author

I always love prodigal son stories, so when Zax first appeared in *A Beautiful Mess*, I knew he had to have his own book. It's stories like Zax's that show no matter what our past says, no matter what we've done, Jesus loves us. And even more than that, He calls all the broken to His mission field, whether that be across the seas or in our own neighborhood. Or especially in our own home.

Please know that no matter where you are in life, God loves you! And He sent His son, born in the lowliest of places, to be your Savior!

Have a blessed Christmas!

~ Brenda

COMPANION SHORT STORY TO BROKEN TOGETHER

Broken Noel

BRENDA S. ANDERSON

BROKEN NOEL

Companion Short Story to
Broken Together

Christmas season has always been a time for joy for Thomas Nordberg and his family, but when his wife succumbs to cancer days before Thanksgiving, that joy is buried with her. In his grief, his relationship with his daughter is wounded as well. A gift to another hurting child may be the only thing that restores joy in their lives.

This story originally appeared in
The Mosaic Collection's 2021 Christmas anthology, *The Heart of Christmas*.

Dedication

To all who grieve during the holiday seasons:
know you do not walk this path alone,
and you are loved with an everlasting love.

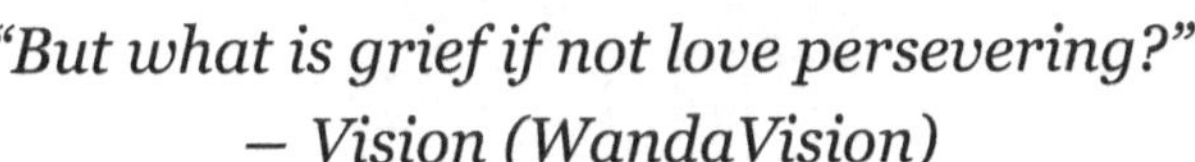

"But what is grief if not love persevering?"
– Vision (WandaVision)

Chapter One

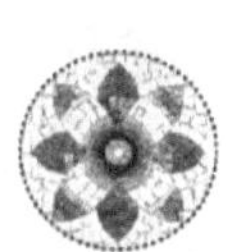

Eight Years Ago
Boston, Massachusetts

Thanksgiving wasn't meant for funerals. At least, that was what he'd argued about with Lacy a week ago, but stubborn woman that she was, she had gotten her wish. And now she was celebrating the holiday with Jesus. Couldn't say that he blamed her. What a way to spend Thanksgiving!

For her, anyway.

Thomas Nordberg blinked back tears as he squeezed his daughter's hand. She leaned into him as the mourners sang along with "It Is Well with My Soul." Lyrics penned by Horatio G. Spafford back in the 1800s following the tragic loss of his four daughters at sea. If Spafford could find peace after their deaths, certainly Thomas would after Lacy's.

His voice clogged as he attempted to sing along. Beside

him, Noelle whispered to the song, trying to be brave. No, he took that back. At only eight years old, she *was* brave, perhaps more than he.

The music changed and the congregation sang Chris Tomlin's version of "Joy to the World." But pain squeezed all the joy from his heart. Sure, he understood Lacy's reasons for picking this song for today. She'd wanted everyone to know the joy of the Lord. But how could he rejoice when Lacy had been amputated from his heart, leaving a gaping wound that might never heal?

He blocked out the song, the lyrics, the people singing behind him. That was the only way he could get through this day. In the courtroom, he was renowned for being an attentive listener and observer—one who didn't miss eyes glancing left, clenched hands, tapping feet. But today, everything was foggy. A numbness in his soul from Lacy's being extracted from his life, like someone might feel if they lost an arm or leg. She had been equally a part of his life.

The song ended, and Pastor Jacob walked in front of the altar. He nodded to Thomas and Noelle and began. "Lacy . . ." He cleared his throat, likely clogged with his own tears, then started again. "I grew up with Lacy Donnellan, presided over her marriage to Thomas." He looked directly at Noelle. "Am Noelle's godfather."

He continued, speaking about her unshakable faith when lung cancer handed her a death sentence. Oh, Thomas had petitioned God, laid down a strong argument for healing, claiming Lacy hadn't even rebelliously tried one cigarette, but facts hadn't mattered.

How could his vibrant, life-loving, Jesus-worshipping wife be dead?

He sniffled and Noelle leaned against him, adding her sniffles to his. He braced an arm around her shoulder as family and friends stood to tell stories about Lacy, all praising her love for him and Noelle, her dogged determination when she pursued anything, her advocacy for victims of violent crimes. No defense attorney wanted to go against prosecutor Lacy Donnellan-Nordberg.

She'd bested him in court during their first meeting.

Then he'd courted her. He smiled at the memory of that whirlwind year.

Guilt nicked his heart for smiling.

What he'd give to go home, sleep, and wake up in the morning to discover this past year of useless chemo and radiation had only been a nightmare.

He shook his head and refocused on Pastor Jacob as he wiped his own tears. Yet the pastor smiled as he looked upward. "Can't wait to hug you in Heaven, Lacy."

Sorrow clogged Thomas's throat, and his empty arms weighed heavy at his side. What he'd give to hug her right now.

He hugged her mini-me instead. Kissed Noelle's forehead. "How are you doing, Chestnut?"

"I miss Mommy."

"I do too." Had it only been four days since she'd made him promise to make the Christmas season a special one for their Christmas-born child? That felt equally like forever and only moments ago.

How could he make the season special? That had been Lacy's department. He'd just replied "Yes, dear" to all her ideas; anything to make her happy. Which, in turn, made him happy. His one regret had been agreeing to that ghastly inflatable Rudolph in the front yard. Oh, he'd hated that thing, which made Lacy love it all the more. She'd loved needling him.

Now who would he argue with, other than attorneys? Making up with them wasn't nearly as enjoyable.

"Daddy." Noelle tugged at his arm. "They want us to go."

What? He looked to his right. Oh. The usher waited at the end of the pew, a sympathetic smile on his face. Thomas stood and took Noelle's hand. Led her down the aisle—the casket was already near the lobby—his focus on the carpet. Nearly every pew in this century-old church was filled with friends and family he refused to break down in front of. Especially colleagues he couldn't show weakness to. Though when someone was interrogated on the stand, if they didn't show emotion befitting the situation, the jury often held that against them.

Now, he intimately understood the need to hold it together. If he started crying, there was no guarantee he would ever stop. Someday, he'd watch a video of the service Lacy had requested they record, not as some macabre reminder, but she'd anticipated his foggy brain, which he'd denied.

No one knew him better than Lacy.

The pallbearers took a right at the bottom of the step, rolling the casket bearing the empty shell of Lacy's body out the door, heading to the cremator.

Thomas veered left, and led the way downstairs to a dining hall that could fit several hundred people. Lacy had chosen this building—not their home church—because of that. She hadn't expected a full church, though she should have with the other guests she planned for that were now lined up by the table.

Lacy wouldn't think of having a Thanksgiving meal without inviting the hungry and the homeless. Just like every Thanksgiving of their married life.

He didn't go to the end of the line, or the front. Instead, he and Noelle detoured into the restrooms to wash their hands, then they walked to the other side of the serving tables. Someone handed each of them an apron, and they took their places by the turkey and mashed potato warmers. Both his parents and Lacy's followed suit and went to their assigned stations, along with a couple of friends. They'd feed the homeless first, then those who had attended the funeral . . . er . . . life celebration.

This, he'd looked forward to. The best way to clear the fog numbing his brain was by serving others, especially those with sadder stories than his own. At least he had a warm home to go to, a daughter to care for, a fridge full of food. Too much food, actually.

The line began moving forward. He forked turkey and laid it on their plates, looking into the eyes of people broken by so many different circumstances. He wanted them to know they were seen, that they bore God's image just as much as he did. If funeral attendees grumbled about being served last, well, they could go somewhere else. Today, he wasn't going to take any guff.

It took about fifteen minutes to reach those who were here to remember Lacy. Suddenly, making eye contact was no longer easy, but he forced himself to greet everyone and thank them for coming. Most said something about missing Lacy. Others commented about her being with Jesus. Then there were the "I'm sorry for your loss" statements.

His warmer had only a few slices left, so he turned to the kitchen. "Any more turkey?"

"Coming right up." One of the church ladies hurried from the kitchen with a refilled tray, and another removed the empty one.

"Thank you for serving," he said to both.

"Pshaw." The woman with blue-gray curls waved her hand. "Anything for our Lacy. Thank you for continuing her tradition. You know she'd be proud."

"I do know that." He refocused on the guests in front of him. Oh joy.

"You let those people go first?" His know-it-all older sister wrinkled her nose and nodded toward the side of the room where most of the homeless sat.

"They were thankful."

Denise grunted and rolled her eyes so vigorously, he thought they'd roll right out of her head and bounce on the floor. One would think a woman nearing forty would have lost that skill, but she'd perfected it into an art form. He wasn't an outgoing person, but he still tended to get along decently with everyone. His sister definitely didn't fit into that category. Standing behind the table alongside him would have done her good.

"How are you doing, Noelle?" At least Denise was kind to her only niece.

Noelle just shrugged. His talkative daughter seemed to have lost her voice.

"It'll get better, sweetie. I promise."

It would. He knew that, but it didn't hurt Noelle to hear the reminder.

"Thank you," he said, to offer Denise kindness. Perhaps it should start with him.

But she looked back at him, her lips in a tight line that showed no wrinkles. Botox had effectively taken care of that. "The program says you're cremating her?"

"We are," he said curtly, then smiled at the next person in line as he forked white meat for them.

"Hmm."

He wasn't going to take the bait. Wasn't going to ask what she meant by that. Instead, he concentrated on greeting the next guest.

"Please don't tell me you're going to keep her urn on the fireplace mantel."

He gritted his teeth, trying to resist the urge to talk back, but his mouth had a different idea. "Yep. On the mantel during the day and my dresser at night." What was it about Denise that made him revert to his twelve-year-old self?

Still, the horrified look on her face was worth it.

Until Noelle elbowed him, and whispered, "Daddy," not so quietly, and in a tone too reminiscent of her mother's.

The word had its desired effect, and he offered his sister a fake smile while clamping his mouth shut.

"Mommy's going to have her ashes buried in a memorial forest." It was just like Noelle to take over. "She found the perfect maple tree overlooking the river, and next spring, we'll mix her ashes with the soil. They'll even have a little plaque by the tree with her name and favorite verse."

Denise's pursed lips indicated she wasn't thrilled with them going a nontraditional route, but at least she kept those lips closed.

"They'll even plant a bunch of saplings in Mommy's honor, and if Daddy ever allows me to get a dog . . ." Noelle raised a single eyebrow with amazing dexterity, like her mother. "Then we can bury our dog's ashes there someday too."

"Sounds . . . interesting."

In other words, she hated the idea. Guess that was *her* problem.

But at least that explanation prompted her to move on. He looked up in relief to see his next-door neighbor holding her plate up for turkey.

"I think it's a splendid idea." Mrs. Rossi frowned at the small slice Thomas laid on her plate. "Just a wee bit more, if you please."

Thomas picked up a larger piece, and she nodded.

"Your Lacy always did treat God's creation with special care. No surprise she wishes to be buried among it."

"She was thrilled when she learned of the forest. She never liked the idea of taking up space in a cemetery."

"I might have to look into that myself, although my Anthony might get lonely, God rest his soul." She held her plate out for potatoes. "Put them right on top of the turkey, thank you." Before moving on for gravy, she looked back at Thomas. "Now I expect you to visit like your Lacy did. She kept me from being too lonely. And a visit with me might chase your loneliness as well."

"Thank you, Mrs. Rossi. I will do that." And he would. Just not right away.

By the time all the ceremony guests had been served, the homeless contingent was coming back for more. His stomach growled, proving to his head he was hungry, though eating held little appeal.

"You go now, Thomas, Noelle." One of the church ladies snuck the fork from his hand. "It's a good thing to keep your stomach full when you grieve."

"Thank you, Ms. . . ."

"Mrs. Garcia. And don't forget to take one of my desserts. The apple crumble is my specialty."

"I'll be sure to try it." He removed his apron and handed it to another woman who was eager to make things easier for him and Noelle, then the two of them walked to the end of the line. If no food was left by the time they reached the buffet table, he'd be fine with that.

"Daddy." Noelle took his hand and began swinging their arms like they used to when she was younger. "Do you think we can check out the Blessing Tree at church on Sunday? I want to start looking for presents."

Thomas froze. Buying gifts for prisoners' children had become an annual tradition, one their family had done together since he married, but he'd hoped Noelle wouldn't bring it up. It would be one more reminder of what he'd lost.

But he had a plan if she did mention it. "How about we start a new tradition this year?"

Her hand went limp in his, but she'd love his idea. "Why don't you and I head to Hawaii instead? I've taken the month off." Actually, the Guilt-Free Project Organization had made him take it off. "We can get away from the cold." He faked a shiver. With the island's warm temps, they could easily forget the Christmas season altogether. Next year, he'd be ready to celebrate again.

But her hand remained limp, then she tugged it away.

He looked down at her, arms crossed, bottom lip stuck out far enough to take a dive off of. "What's wrong, Chestnut?"

"Blessing Tree's my favorite. It was Mommy's too."

He opened his mouth to object, but then realized that any judge in the world would slam the gavel and say, "Overruled."

"You're right," he finally forced out, though his heart was 95 percent against it. Appeasing Noelle was the other

5 percent, which was far more important. “We can go to church on Sunday and choose a family to adopt.”

“Thank you, Daddy.” Noelle wrapped her arms around his waist and hung on. He’d be doing his own clinging on—to his sanity—if Noelle insisted on having a traditional Christmas season though, because everything about Christmas would remind him of Lacy.

Chapter Two

"Daddy, Daddy, where are you?"

Thomas forced his eyes open, saw the sun sneaking beneath the shade, then jerked up in bed. Where was he? He blinked to awaken his vision while reaching for his glasses on the nightstand. Wait, where was the nightstand?

"Daddy?" She knocked on the door.

"I'm in here." The morning haze cleared from his brain. *Here*, being the guest room. He covered up with a blanket and spied his glasses on the bedstand on the other side of the bed. "Come on in."

The door flew open, and Noelle rushed in, leaped up on the bed, hugged her arms tightly around his neck. "I was so worried."

"I'm sorry, Chestnut. I needed to try something else." After six sleepless nights in the master, reaching for his wife, who wasn't there—would never be there—he'd made the move to the guest room. Having slept through the night, clearly the change had worked, but it also had frightened his daughter.

"Are you okay?" He peeled her arms from his neck and looked her in the eye.

"I am now."

"Good." He patted the space beside him, and she snuggled in like she used to do with Lacy. Once, he'd been jealous of that closeness, but now he realized how petty that had been. He'd give anything to have Lacy back. Why God chose to take her . . . He could have healed her if He'd wanted to.

An unfamiliar emotion tightened his muscles, and it even felt good. Maybe it just felt good to feel, period.

"Something wrong, Daddy?"

He circled a hand over Noelle's back, pondering his response. Lacy had advised him to always be truthful to Noelle, as it would encourage her to open up as well, but to measure his words according to her age. What that meant, he wasn't even sure. All he could do was try. In a different time, he would have asked God for help finding the right words, but how do you seek help from someone you're angry with?

"I'm struggling, Chestnut." His hand stilled. "I know God is always good, but I'm not happy with Him right now."

"I understand. I'm not happy either." She leaned even tighter and wrapped her arms around him. "I just want Mommy back."

"Same here, sweetheart. Same here."

They sat there, holding each other, as time slid by with quiet efficiency. Thomas eventually glanced at the clock on the bedstand on the opposite side of the bed, but the numbers blurred without his glasses, which were folded up in front of the clock.

He hated disturbing their silence, but the OCD in him needed to know the time. “Noelle, can you read the clock?”

“Nine twenty-two.” Precise, just like her parents. Then she pulled away from him and retrieved his glasses.

He slid them on, and the world came into focus. “Much better.”

“I ate cereal already.” She climbed from the bed. “So I’ll get ready for church.” She hurried from the room as if church would solve all her woes.

He’d hoped Noelle would have forgotten his promise and want to stay home, but he couldn’t disappoint her. He got out of bed, scratched his scruffy face that hadn’t felt a razor since Thanksgiving morning. They’d missed the nine-a.m. service, the one they usually attended, but could easily make the eleven.

Still, at the moment, he had no desire to go to church and fake a smile. Perhaps he should leave his blond and graying whiskers, then he wouldn’t have to pretend he wasn’t angry. What he’d give to find a church that didn’t require you to leave your baggage at the door. Pastor Jacob claimed this one didn’t, but Thomas couldn’t recall ever seeing someone who looked broken.

Or maybe he hadn’t been paying attention.

Guess today, his eyes would be opened.

He made the bed and left the guest room for the master, skipping both the kitchen and breakfast. Maybe his appetite would return someday, but food only served one purpose: fuel to keep putting one foot in front of the other. He showered, shaved, then dressed in jeans and a sweater. Lacy always liked them to dress up. Today, he didn't care.

That give him a few minutes to check the newspaper. He gathered it from the steps, and his gut twisted at the headline. "King Stockett Gets Life in Prison." Lacy's last case—one that had probably hastened her death.

Thomas had never been a proponent of the death penalty, but for a man this evil? On one drug-filled evening, he'd murdered every member of his family—his wife and three children—except for a daughter who was visiting a friend. It was that daughter who discovered the bodies.

So Stockett got to live, and Lacy didn't.

Thomas slammed his fist on the table and spewed a word he rarely used.

"Something wrong, Daddy?" Noelle peeked in the kitchen but didn't enter.

No doubt, he'd frightened her.

God, please forgive me.

Honestly, he'd frightened himself, but he needed to make it up to Noelle.

"I'm sorry." He patted the chair beside him, and she hesitantly made her way to sit. "I'm . . . angry, and I said a naughty word. Will you forgive me?"

She nibbled on her lower lip and nodded.

"Thank you, Chestnut." He hugged her extra-long to assure her he wasn't angry with her.

She squirmed from his grasp. "Can I go back to my book now?"

"Of course."

She kissed him on the cheek and scurried into the living room, her worry replaced with a smile. How easily she forgave. If only it were that easy for him.

He made a cup of coffee in his Keurig, hoping that would calm the rage still churning in his gut.

By ten thirty, his temper had cooled to a light simmer.

He left the kitchen and motioned to his daughter, who sat reading on the couch. "Time to go."

"Yay!" She marked her spot with a bookmark then leaped from the couch.

What he'd give to summon half of her joy.

He pulled her jacket from the closet and selected a light jacket for himself as the temps were hovering just below forty today. With the way he was feeling, though, he might not even need the coat.

In his Mercedes, Noelle turned on the radio and found Christmas music. "O Holy Night," one of Lacy's favorites.

A tear nicked the corner of his eye, and he blinked it away. Was every little thing this month going to remind him of Lacy? If not for Noelle, he'd find a different station, one that didn't care that Advent began today and that Christians around the world were preparing for the celebration of Jesus's birth.

He parked at the church that had transformed since the last time he'd attended, two weeks ago now. If only he'd known then, as he'd pushed Lacy in her wheelchair through the front doors, that she wouldn't live to see it decked out for Christmas, maybe he would have encouraged the church to decorate early. Now the white twinkling lights on the building and the trees surrounding it mocked him. What he'd give to turn around and go home. If only Noelle would agree to leave the state. The country. Go somewhere he and Lacy hadn't spent time at, so there would be no reminders.

But that wasn't what Noelle wanted, and he needed to make her happy.

He took her hand as they walked to the church, and that quelled some of the rustling in his stomach. Normally, she would have shaken him off, claiming she was too old. For this one small thing, he gave thanks. He kept his head down as they entered the building. In the middle of the foyer, there stood the Blessing Tree. It couldn't be avoided, and no surprise, Noelle ran right to it.

While he forced his feet to move forward.

A few tags remained on the tree that had been up since the first part of November. All the tags had children's names on them, children who had a parent in prison. But at least they had that parent. Noelle would never see her mom again, never receive a gift from her or even a note. And all Lacy had done was serve others.

He glanced at a tag, and his fists balled up on their own, it seemed, desiring to punch something. He couldn't do this. “Chestnut, go ahead and choose a name. I need to go to the restroom.” Usually, they’d go through the names together, pray over them, choose two or three to adopt, then they’d shop together. But today, he couldn’t help Noelle choose.

“But Daddy . . .” He didn’t need to see her face to know her smile fell as he hurried off, but he’d rather deal with her disappointment than the feelings bubbling inside himself. He stopped at a water fountain on the way to the restroom, and gulped water until he felt as if he could drown in it.

“Hey, you should slow down.”

Thomas felt a hand on his back and straightened to glower over the much shorter Pastor Jacob.

“I’m sorry you have to go through this.” The pastor looked up into Thomas’s eyes with so much compassion, he couldn’t help but look away.

“Yeah.” Thomas wiped a hand over his mouth. “Me too.”

The pastor gestured toward an empty table in the fellowship hall. “Got a moment?”

“Sure.” Thomas glanced down the hallway to where Noelle stood by the tree.

She looked up and saw him, and he gestured toward the table, indicating she’d find him there. She nodded, then kept doing her research. To her, choosing a name meant looking at each tag, praying over it, and listening for an answer.

The pastor brought two cups of coffee and a couple of

Christmas cookies to the table. “Lacy told me to make sure you eat, even if it’s sugar.”

“Of course, she did.” He dunked his cookie in the coffee and took a bite. It actually made him hungry for more.

“You realize it’s okay to skip church once in a while, though I’m glad to see you here.”

“Well, if it weren’t for Noelle needing to pick a child’s name, we probably wouldn’t be here.”

“Interesting what vessels God uses, isn’t it?”

Sure. Whatever. Thomas dunked and ate the rest of his cookie. Wouldn’t mind having another one.

“I’ll get more.” The pastor leaped up as if he’d read Thomas’s mind. Who knew, maybe he had. In the courtroom, Thomas easily read people, so maybe here it was the same for Pastor Jacob.

He returned with a plateful of sweets, looking a little sheepish. “Belinda gave me a hard time for being greedy, but I told her it was important for the ministry.”

“That’s the truth.” The treats had actually calmed him, so he grabbed a couple more. Then he checked his watch. Just a few minutes until the eleven o’clock service started. “If you need to go on in, I don’t mind catching up with you afterward.” If he stuck around.

“William’s preaching today. I’ve got baggage duty.”

“Baggage duty?”

“Yep. If I spot anyone lugging around their baggage—which really is everyone here, if you want the truth—I stop and chat. You looked like you needed a listening ear.”

Yet, Pastor Jacob had done all the talking so far.

Thomas smirked at that thought. He'd keep quiet, and see how long it took the reverend to listen.

Both men grabbed another cookie, sipped their coffee, found a non-dirty spot on the table to scratch at.

Okay, so Pastor Jacob did want to listen. Well, in that case, Thomas planned to do a whole bunch of unpacking. The problem with unpacking was, then you had to put things away, even if that meant placing it in the dirty laundry. Which in turn needed to be cleaned. He didn't have the strength for it.

Thomas picked at that same non-dirty spot on the table. "King Stockett was sentenced to life."

"Ah, yes, I'd heard that."

"Lacy spent the last year of her life making sure he wouldn't see the light of day. Probably stole months off her life. It's not right."

"No." Pastor Jacob shook his head. "It isn't."

"And I know life isn't fair. Quote that to Noelle all the time, but I try my best to even it out, get people out of prison who aren't guilty." He ran a hand down his face. "Somehow it feels different when you're personally affected."

"It certainly does."

"All this . . ." Thomas held up clenched fists. "It's irrational." Generally, he wasn't an angry person, and was at a loss as to how to deal with it.

"And it's a very normal stage of grief."

A stage of grief . . . He hadn't considered that.

"May I make a suggestion?"

"Please do." Thomas hated this feeling and feared he might lash out at Noelle, more than the ugly word she'd heard from him this morning.

"When someone commits a crime, don't lawyers have some form they write up with their legal argument?"

"Yes, a petition."

"Well, do that. Spill your anger out in a petition, whatever that looks like to you."

That wasn't a bad idea. He grabbed another cookie from the plate and nibbled on it. Yeah, he'd write a petition, laying out his argument against God for taking Lacy too early. His mind already churned with the wording.

"Daddy?"

Thomas spun to his daughter, who held a single tag in her hand. "I only chose one because I know this is tough on you."

"Oh, Chestnut." He gathered her in his arms and kissed her hair. "You choose as many as you want, okay? We'll be all right."

"Well . . ." She pulled away, looked down at the tag, nibbled on her lower lip, then peered up at Thomas. "I prayed over every one, like you and Mommy taught me, but this is the only one that I heard a *Yes* for."

"Then that's the one we'll choose. I trust you chose well."

A smile he hadn't seen in over a week blossomed on her face. It even managed to chase away some of his resentment.

"May I see it, please?"

Noelle held it against her heart. "She's an eight-year-old, like me. And she wants books and science kits, like me." She handed him the tag.

And Thomas's stomach flip flopped.

One detail Noelle had neglected to share was the child's name, Princess Paris. No last name was given, but Thomas had no doubt it was Stockett and that she was the surviving daughter of convicted murderer King Stockett, the man who'd shortened Lacy's life.

Chapter Three

Thomas dated and digitally signed the petition and saved the file, only ten days after Pastor Jacob had given him the assignment. He'd spent time each day in his home office, pouring his heart and anger into the petition, listing every reason he could think of to tell God He'd made a huge mistake in taking Lacy. He hadn't held back. The pastor had been smart giving him this assignment—it had been cleansing.

He closed his laptop with a sense of vindication.

Followed by a stab of guilt. Who was he to petition the Righteous Judge, the Lawgiver, our King! And tell Him He was guilty of sentencing the wrong person? Talk about hubris.

Although he wasn't terribly sorry about his suggestion that God trade King Stockett for Lacy. He'd only been half kidding.

Regardless, the anger he'd experienced ten days ago had abated, much to his relief, though his emotions were still unstable. Now it was time to do another type of writing he should have tackled right away but procrastinated. Not his typical conduct, but Lacy's death had brought out strange behaviors.

He retrieved the overfull boxes of sympathy and thank-you cards from his office credenza and lugged them to the dining room. By the time he was done writing, his hand would probably never be the same. Little was done anymore with a regular pen and paper.

He called up the stairs, asking Noelle to come down, then he returned to his office to retrieve the guest book, pens, address labels, and stamps. Hopefully, that would be all that was required.

"Finally." Noelle waited by the table, her arms crossed, tapping her foot on the hardwood, looking too much like her mother when Lacy had an issue with something he'd done wrong. He never had learned to handle that properly.

"Just finished a petition." Not admitting that the petition was a personal matter niggled at him a bit, but she wouldn't understand what he'd had to do and why. "Now, the goal is to write twenty thank-yous a day." At that rate, they should be done by Christmas.

"Then we can go shopping?"

"Yes." He nodded. Though the idea of shopping for King's daughter still made his stomach churn. "I'll write the note in the cards and address the envelopes. You get to sign your name, put on the stamp and the return address labels. The more we work together, the quicker we get it all done."

"Fine."

He sat on one side of the table, placed the guest book above his writing space, the sympathy cards to his left, and the empty thank-you cards to his right. An efficient layout would help speed up their progress.

"Done yet?" Noelle sat across from him and rolled her eyes. Oh, this attitude was a new one from his daughter, but then his attitude was evolving as well. Would they ever go back to normal? What was normal now, anyway?

If only Lacy hadn't taken on the case this year—if only Thomas had put his foot down and demanded she prioritize her health—maybe the cancer wouldn't have been so aggressive. Maybe it could have been cured, or at least her life prolonged.

If only God had prioritized her over King Stockett.

He scribbled a quick note to someone who'd sent twenty dollars. All the money would go to the foundation he and Lacy had begun years ago to help the families of people who'd been wrongly incarcerated.

That certainly wasn't King Stockett. And now Thomas had to buy King's daughter a gift. Not that it was her fault that her father was an evil man, but someone else would take care of her. He knew that from volunteering with the Blessing Tree organization for many years. No child was left out.

But choosing someone else would hurt Noelle, so he stuffed his feelings down where they would have less chance of resurfacing, and continued with the thank-you chore.

Over an hour later, they finished their first group of twenty, which meant it was time to fight the crowds at the mall. Not his favorite task, nor his favorite place anytime, much less during Christmas shopping season.

Noelle ran upstairs to change into mall-appropriate attire, whatever that was. All he cared was that she dressed modestly. He'd make her run right up and change if he didn't approve.

Oh, he was a grump, and no doubt, that was affecting Noelle.

God, help me make it through today.

A prayer? Wow. When was the last time he'd thought to seek God's help? When was the last time he'd spoken with God other than the rote prayers at church or yelling at Him through the petition?

Lacy would be so disappointed in him. Well, if she hadn't insisted on working so much, maybe she'd be here to whip him back into shape.

Oy, what a mess he was. He retrieved his coat from the entry closet and slipped his feet into winter shoes. He'd always prided himself on being even keeled, but this had completely knocked him off his center. And if that could happen, had his center really been God?

That was a question worth exploring.

But right now, he had the privilege of shopping with his daughter. Yes, it was a privilege, even if he didn't want to go.

Lacy thundered downstairs wearing leggings, a T-shirt, and a jean jacket. Good enough, he guessed.

"Ready to go?" He held her winter jacket out to her.

And she actually smiled. He'd seen that expression so rarely in the past two and a half weeks. Had it been that long since Lacy had gone to Jesus?

He stuffed down the thought and gestured toward the door leading into the garage. Noelle bounded out with an enthusiasm he wished he had.

"Are we going out to eat afterward?" She spun back toward him as he locked the door. "Mommy would always take me out."

"Sure. Your choice." Finally, a task he was glad to say yes to. They'd survived on hot dishes—Lacy would have called them casseroles—from caring neighbors and church friends, but what he really wanted was a steak. For that, he was hungry.

She named one of their favorite local restaurants, one they'd frequently gone to as a family. It wouldn't be the same without Lacy, but then, what was?

After a half-hour drive, they arrived at the mall and found a parking spot about as far away from an entrance as they could get. Guess they'd both be getting in their walking today. At least they weren't trudging through snow.

"Where to first?" he said as they finally reached the entrance.

"Bookstore."

Which meant they were going to be a while. Not a complaint. Though he had to be cautious with what Noelle chose. Being at an eighth-grade reading level in third grade made books her age boring, but he and Lacy had discovered that books geared toward thirteen- and fourteen-year-olds were fraught with problems. Too many had teen romance, and that romance was far more advanced than any thirteen-year-old should read, much less an eight-year-old. Then there was the cursing allowed in books, language Noelle would normally not hear at home, though others probably did.

Still, he gave her some freedom to browse, with her never really out of his line of sight. Which also meant he had to browse in whatever section allowed him to keep an eye on her. He'd found many interesting books that way, ones he never would have intentionally searched for.

Noelle stopped in front of preteen reads, so he parked himself two rows away. "You've got to be kidding me," he mumbled as he stared at the rows of books on death, grief, and bereavement. God really had great timing.

"Pardon me?" A woman from across the aisle glanced his way.

He shook his head. "Sorry, just talking to myself." His dad would have told him he was having an intelligent conversation.

The woman angled toward him. "Aww, that's a tough section to be looking through."

Tell me about it.

"You've lost someone recently?"

"My wife," he said, though he wasn't sure why he shared that. It was none of her business.

"I'm very sorry. My husband passed nearly twenty

years ago, and I still miss him."

Not exactly an encouraging thought. How many people had told him that time would soften the loss? Part of him never wanted to stop hurting because that would suggest he was moving on. Maybe he didn't want to move on.

Which meant he needed to move from this section. "What are you looking for?"

"Just trying to get some Christmas craft ideas."

He glanced at the section in front of her. Holiday. He sighed. God might be nudging him, but Thomas refused to listen. Time to do a little nudging of his own, get Noelle to make a choice so they could move on. He forced out the words. "Hope you have a merry Christmas."

"Why thank you. And you, too."

Well, that wasn't going to happen, but he smiled and glanced in Noelle's direction. A dozen heads bobbed between them, but being well over six feet, he could see above them.

And his blood ran cold.

Where was she?

Don't panic. She moved on to another section while you were distracted. He shuffled between other book shoppers, apologizing as he bumped them, but he didn't stop. He reached the end of the aisle then walked past the endcaps, where he could scan each aisle and see right into the mall. An overcrowded mall where anyone could hide.

Or where a trafficker could easily slip away. One of the problems of being an attorney was that he often worked with the dregs of this life, so it didn't take much for his imagination to head down the worst routes.

He jostled between the shoppers, calling out, "Noelle" as he aimed toward the checkout lane. People skewered him with their eyes as he elbowed his way to the front of the line, but he had no choice. Even the teen at the register gave him a who-do-you-think-you-are sneer when he cut in front of an elderly woman without apologizing.

"My daughter is missing," he said breathlessly, suddenly realizing his heart was beating in overdrive. "Please notify the mall security."

"Did you try calling her?" The teen rolled her eyes as if he were stupid.

"Call security. Now." He would have called Noelle if she had a phone, but neither he nor Lacy figured a preteen needed one.

Had they been wrong?

No time for second guessing right now. That would come later. He took out his own phone, showed the clerk a picture he'd taken of Noelle before entering the mall. Another safeguard in case something like this happened. That way, he could easily describe what Noelle was wearing and show an updated photo.

While the clerk made the call, he held up the picture of Noelle to the shoppers. "Has anyone seen my daughter? She was in this store just a minute ago."

Until that woman distracted him . . .

Had that been her plan? Oftentimes traffickers worked in tandem. One distracted the parent while the other got away with the child. Thomas knew this, but he'd still let

Noelle out of his sight. He never should have come to the mall in the first place, not when he was so unfocused.

"Please." He gulped, doing his best to not break down in front of the world. "Help me find my daughter."

If something happened to her, he'd never forgive himself.

Chapter Four

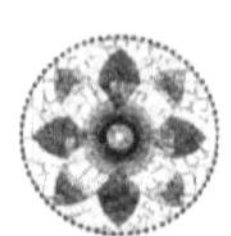

Thomas stood in the middle of the shopping crowd, holding his phone in the air. A few people murmured, some shook their heads, others talked among themselves or ignored him altogether. Another reason why he shouldn't have lost focus. People were too absorbed in their own little worlds to notice what went on around them.

Just like him today. He had to snap out of this, whatever *this* was.

Security finally arrived, after what seemed an eternity. He showed them her picture, told them where she'd been when he'd last seen her. They did a lot of talking back and forth on their two-way radios. They knew what they were doing—they dealt with stuff like this all the time—but not with his daughter.

"You're looking pale." One of the officers directed him to a chair. "Have a seat."

He obeyed without arguing. The dad in him wanted to

get up and join the search, but the attorney in him knew that would only complicate matters. It was best he stay put.

Someone handed him a water, which he gulped down.

"Anything?" He looked up at an officer as she put down her radio.

She shook her head.

Someone placed their hand on his shoulder, and he heard unintelligible whispers. He glanced behind him.

Strangers were praying.

And he hadn't given it a thought. If God was testing him, He'd find Thomas sorely lacking.

So he steepled his hands together, rested his forehead on them, and beseeched God's forgiveness for his inability to see beyond himself, for railing at God and not inviting Him into this period of grief. Then he pleaded with God to find Noelle. He promised to spend more time in prayer and reading the Bible, things he'd prioritized before Lacy died.

And yet, she'd still died.

No, he couldn't think like that. If he had faith—

"Daddy?"

Noelle? He opened his eyes and spotted her in the entry beside a security guard. He leaped from his chair and reached her in two long strides. "Chestnut." He enfolded her in his arms and never wanted to let go.

"Daddy, I can't breathe."

Oh. "Sorry, sweetheart." He loosened his grip but didn't completely release her. "Where were you? What happened?"

The officer accompanying her cleared her throat. "She was in the restroom."

He drew back—noticing a crowd had gathered around them—keeping his hands on her shoulders. "You were where?"

Noelle looked toward the floor. "You were busy talking, and I had to go bad. I figured I'd be back in time, but the bathrooms were on the other side of the mall . . ."

He mentally counted to ten, reining in his frustration. She knew she wasn't supposed to go anywhere without him. It had been drilled into her.

"You scared me to death." He took her back in his arms as the onlookers dispersed, probably disappointed they hadn't witnessed breaking news.

"I'm sorry, Daddy. I won't do it again."

"I trust you won't." He took her hand, needing to head away from this bedlam. "Let's go home."

She tugged her hand free. "But I haven't bought the presents yet."

Again, he counted to ten, debating how to respond. If they didn't finish shopping now, that just meant delaying the inevitable.

"Okay, choose your books, but I'm not leaving your side."

"Thank you, Daddy."

She shouldn't thank him yet, because once they got home, she'd receive her punishment. No doubt it would be one she wouldn't like at all.

"You're grounded until Christmas."

"But Daddy—"

"No buts. You disobeyed the rules, and there are consequences for that." Thomas sat across the dining room table from his pouting daughter. He hated meting out punishment, but he knew from working with the justice system that when punishment was withheld, society paid a price. There were times when grace was effective, but that was determined by case. Too often when a judge went light on the sentence, an innocent paid the price.

In this case, Noelle needed to be punished, so her going somewhere without notifying him would never happen again.

She got up and stomped her foot on the hardwood. "You're just an old meanie."

Yeah, he knew that. Parenting had been so much easier when he'd had Lacy to back him up. He wasn't as gentle with words as Lacy, either. She could dole out punishment, and Noelle would accept it. But him? He received backlash.

"If you sit down, we can work on some more thank-yous, then you and I can do something fun together."

"I don't wanna do anything with you." She crossed her arms and stomped from the dining room all the way upstairs to her bedroom, where she slammed the door loud enough for the neighbors to hear.

Lacy, how would you handle this?

Should he go upstairs and inform her that her behavior

was unacceptable? Or should this be one of those moments of grace? If only Lacy were here to give an answer.

He settled on the latter, mostly to avoid more preteen drama. Working with adults was much easier. They were far more predictable.

So he sat at the dining room table and filled out thank-you cards until his entire forearm hurt. Then he caught up on what was happening at work. No, they didn't need him. He watched the news, but that only left him depressed. He tried rereading one of his favorite books, but even that left him empty.

Just like this house.

Maybe they should move.

Or maybe that would be too many changes and losses for Noelle.

And now, when he was emotionally, mentally, and spiritually depleted, was definitely not the time to make a life-altering decision. Good thing he had still the wisdom to realize that. Perhaps the best plan, then, was to take a nap. While his dreams weren't empty of problems, at least there he wasn't continually wondering what he could have done to save Lacy. Or how he would survive without her.

He took the steps to the second floor, heading for the master. He stopped in the doorway and stared at the bed dressed in linens Lacy had chosen, at the walls wearing wallpaper she'd painstakingly picked out, at the furniture they'd chosen together that anchored the room. He couldn't enter.

Instead, he headed across the hall to the guest room

where he'd spent the last ten days. This room had also been decorated by Lacy, but not specifically for the two of them. Perhaps this was where he was meant to be.

He retrieved a blanket from the closet, lay down on top of the duvet, closed his eyes, and prayed for mind-numbing sleep.

For the next seven days, he repeated the pattern. Argue with Noelle, usually over decorating for Christmas. Write thank-you notes until his hand hurt. Check in with work. Watch the news. Take a nap.

With each day, the naps grew longer.

"Dad?" Noelle knocked on the open door, and he opened one eye to peek at her, then realized something drastic had changed between them.

She'd called him Dad, not Daddy.

He wiped his eyes and sat up in bed. Patted the space beside him. "What's up, Chestnut?"

She remained beneath the doorframe, as if afraid to enter. Not that he could blame her, the way he'd acted toward her these past weeks. It was as though his body had been invaded by an alien, and he was unable to alter his behavior.

"I'm sorry for how I've been acting." He patted the bed again. "I promise, I won't bite."

She lingered a moment longer then entered cautiously and climbed up on the bed. But she didn't snuggle like his eight-year-old should have.

"Why are you in here all the time instead of your own room?" A deep sadness filled her voice.

His answer wasn't easy, so he pondered his words before setting them free, settling on the truth, which was always best. "Because I can't go in there without feeling your mother, seeing her, missing her, and I don't get any rest."

"Oh." She moved a little closer to him and reclined against a pillow. "Is that why you won't put up Christmas decorations?"

This child was far too wise. "Yes." That was the simplest answer, though he felt there was more to it that he couldn't name.

She moved closer, but still didn't reach his side. Was she that fearful he'd bark at her or turn her away? "The presents should go to church today."

The presents . . .

Oh, those presents, for the Blessing Tree. For King Stockett's daughter. Yes, today was the deadline for dropping them off at church. Usually, he and Lacy volunteered to help with distribution, but that would mean he might have to face King's daughter, and that was something he couldn't do with civility.

"Can we go?"

"Of course." He tried to smile, tried to show enthusiasm, but failed.

Still, Noelle bounced from the room, and he met her in the living room. She'd retrieved the bags of gifts from his office and set them by the garage door. They weren't to be wrapped, so the organizers could determine if a gift was appropriate or not. Instead, he and Noelle placed them in a large red gift bag.

Though Blessing Tree asked that each child receive at least three presents, Princess Paris had hit the jackpot. Noelle had chosen a popular novel for preteens, along with a Bible for girls that even had coloring pages. So, naturally, they had to include colored pencils as well. Noelle had also picked out a robotics kit for Princess while pointing out, for herself, a kit training how to examine patients. Apparently, Noelle's latest career choice was oncologist. Lastly, she chose a winter outfit for Princess. Leggings, top, and socks.

Also, because he couldn't tune out Lacy, he'd purchased a hundred-dollar gift card for the family Princess Paris was staying with. Could be her extended family or a foster family or who knew. Either way, they'd be blessed as well, as Lacy always said. This year, he'd take her word for it.

They both signed a Christmas card and enclosed the gift card with it. Then he attached the Blessing Tree tag, with Princess Paris's name, to the bag.

Done.

That hadn't been so bad. Not once had they fought. Now they just had to drop off the gifts at church. Then he was done for the year. He had no plans to sort or deliver the gifts, as he and Lacy had previously done. Someone else would have that privilege this year.

"Ready?" He carried the gift bag and gestured toward the coat closet.

She practically ran toward it. In record time, she had

on her coat, mittens, hat, and boots and had buckled herself into the front seat of the car. Having his height, she'd graduated from the backseat long ago, but Lacy had insisted she sit in back. So this was one small area in which Noelle actually approved of his decision.

Once at the church, she hustled inside, lugging the bag, and carried it to the tree that reached up to the ceiling. She set the bag among the plethora of others beneath the tree. A lot of children would be blessed this year.

Noelle glanced upward and remained in that pose as he came by her side.

"Is everything okay?" He placed a hand on her shoulder, and she didn't wince. That was progress.

She shrugged. "Just wishing we had a tree."

Yeah, he knew that, but he couldn't bring himself to go tree hunting this year. That was something they'd done as a family.

But he had another idea. "Maybe we should start a new tradition. Get a permanent tree."

Noelle whiplashed into the "Mr. Hyde" half of Jekyll and Hyde. She stomped her foot and pressed out that lower lip. "I want a real tree."

"Let's talk about—"

"Good afternoon, Nordberg family."

His jaw tight, Thomas turned to Pastor Jacob, unable to muster a smile or a good afternoon. "Hello."

Noelle said nothing.

"Thanks for participating again this year."

"Noelle wouldn't have done otherwise." He set a hand

on her shoulder, and she shrugged it off. Back to square one.

"Will you be volunteering at the sorting center? Delivering?"

"Not this year." He folded his arms across his chest, hoping to close off this conversation.

"I'm sorry to hear that."

Thomas could tell what the pastor was doing. Trying to get Thomas involved in something that would take his focus off Lacy.

"Perhaps next year, then." Pastor Jacob knelt beside Noelle. "What did you buy?"

Her eyes lit up as she told him, in detail, about her purchases, along with their mall mishap.

"You must have been frantic." The pastor looked up at Thomas.

"That doesn't begin to describe it." He still hadn't recovered.

The pastor stood. "Know that we're all praying for you."

"I appreciate it." And he did. The power of prayer was still real to him, even though they hadn't received the answer they wanted with Lacy. God had answered with healing. It just hadn't taken place this side of Heaven.

"If you two need anything, please call."

Thomas wasn't to the point of asking for help yet. He and Noelle would get through this, it would just take time.

"I will. Thank you." He turned to go and realized Noelle wasn't following. "You coming, sweetheart?"

"I s'pose." She shuffled toward him, her gaze downcast

as if he were asking her to surrender her favorite book.

Pastor Jacob waved, but his not-so-happy smile betrayed that he read Noelle's body language. What did he expect when a child had lost her mother right before Christmas?

They didn't speak as they walked to the car, and Noelle remained silent until they reached the freeway. "I want to go to Grandma's."

Grandma's? "May I ask why?"

She sat quiet, fiddling with her hands, then said, barely above a whisper. "Because they're celebrating Christmas."

He drummed his fingers on the steering wheel. "We are too, Chestnut. Just differently."

"No, we're not. You won't get a tree. You haven't gone shopping. You won't put up decorations. You don't even read Advent stories."

There were a whole bunch of *you don'ts* in that paragraph. A whole bunch of truth-filled accusations. The kid would make a good attorney.

"And you don't love me anymore."

He skidded onto the shoulder and coaxed the car back onto the blacktop. "Of course, I love you, Chestnut."

"Could've fooled me."

"Sweetheart, we're both having a tough time right now. It'll get better. I promise."

She started crying.

Now what should he do? Say? Maybe a night or two with Grandma and Grandpa would help them both.

"How about this?" He pointed to his phone. "Give

Grandma a call, see if you can stay the night."

"Really?" She hiccuped a sob and sniffled.

"Really."

"Thank you, Daddy."

Well, at least he was back to Daddy again.

She made the call, and of course Lacy's mom welcomed Noelle for as long as she wished to stay. Thomas drove home so Noelle could pack, then he made the half-hour trip to the Donnellans' home. Noelle barely let him hug her before she ran up to her bedroom.

"Things aren't going well?" Laura Donnellan invited—rather, ordered—him to join her in the kitchen for a cup of coffee.

"She's having a difficult time." Thomas sat at the table.

Laura's mouth quivered and her hand shook as she poured coffee into two cups. "She isn't the only one."

"I'm sorry." In his own grief, he hadn't considered that Lacy's parents would be mourning the loss of their only daughter as much as he was.

She handed him a cup, sat across from him, and glanced toward the stairs. "Having Noelle here, a piece of Lacy, will help."

"She won't be a bother?"

Laura poured cream into her cup. "My granddaughter is never a bother."

True. They sat quietly, sipping, neither really knowing what to say. He'd read somewhere that the best thing to say to someone who's grieving is nothing. Providing a listening ear was far more meaningful. In this case, he appreciated someone not offering advice.

Thomas finished his cup of coffee. “Thank you. For everything. Time for me to head home.”

“Without supper?”

“I’ll eat at home.”

“Will you?”

Maybe. Maybe not. He’d always made sure Noelle got fed, which meant he’d eaten with her. “I will.” It was a little lie, but still a lie. Food had lost its taste, and he’d lost all cravings for it.

“Before you go.” She hurried down the hallway and returned with a business card. “Roy and I have been talking with Dr. Wade, and she’s helped.”

He pocketed the card with no intention of using it. “I appreciate it.” He aimed for the front door.

“Thomas.”

He turned back to his mother-in-law.

“We love you.” She opened her arms.

For a second, he hesitated, then accepted her embrace. “I love you, too,” he said, before heading for the door. He hated the relief he felt at leaving Noelle with her grandparents, but he knew that, at this moment, she’d be better off with them than him, and he didn’t know when that would change.

Chapter Five

Thomas inserted the key into the door leading to the house and froze. How had he gotten here? The last thing he was cognizant of was closing the door at his in-laws. Or were they his former in-laws now? How did that work?

Didn't matter. What mattered was that he had no recollection of driving home. That made him no better than someone driving under the influence. He'd been equally dangerous. Thankfully, he'd made it home safely, without hurting anyone else. Perhaps the best thing for him to do now was to sleep off this melancholy.

He let himself into the house, walked through the kitchen, and tried not to notice the dirty dishes in the sink. He tried not thinking about the lack of food in the fridge, other than hot dishes delivered by church ladies. If he never ate another hot dish, that would be too soon. He climbed the stairs and headed right into the guest room, without even contemplating going into the master bedroom.

Before lying down though, he switched the nightstand from the left side to the right so he wouldn't wonder where his glasses and phone were upon waking.

He sat on the bed, and his phone rang just as he was about to turn off the ringer. Should he answer or let it ring? Guess it depended upon who was making the call. If it was Noelle, he wouldn't ignore her.

Not Noelle, but Pastor Jacob.

He hovered his finger over the Ignore button. Was that what this younger generation called ghosting? When it came to current slang, he couldn't keep up. Staying current on ever-changing laws was difficult enough.

The phone rang on, and he finally swiped to answer, though he didn't feel one iota like talking. "This is Thomas."

"I was about to hang up. Glad you answered." The man sounded sickeningly cheery. "This is Pastor Jacob, by the way."

"What do you need, Pastor?" That came out far too gruff. "I'm sorry."

"No apologies necessary. I won't keep you long, and I know we talked earlier today, but I wanted to ask again if you'd be interested in helping with Blessing Tree deliveries. We're running short of volunteers, and I know you have always enjoyed it."

Well, that was before Lacy left them. "Not this year, Pastor, but keep us on the list for next year."

"Was worth a try." Silence, then, "How are you really doing, Thomas?"

Ah, so there was an ulterior motive in him calling. The man was certainly clever. "I'm surviving. Noelle went to stay with Lacy's parents for a day or two." If not more.

"I see."

Counselor-speak for "That could be a problem."

"I'll be fine, Pastor. I just need . . ." What did he need? Time alone? It wasn't as though Noelle occupied much of his time. She'd always been independent, like her parents.

"I understand." And he probably did. "Just know I'm a phone call away. You need me, I'll be there."

"I appreciate it." They said their goodbyes, and Thomas silenced his phone. If Noelle tried calling, he'd call her back. She'd understand. He lay on the duvet, covered himself with a blanket, removed his glasses, and fell into a much-needed sleep.

Ding-dong, ding-dong, ding-dong.

What in the world?

Thomas jerked up in bed as the doorbell continued its incessant dinging. Whoever it was, they were going to get an earful along with a door slammed in their face.

He snatched his glasses from the side table and caught the time. Two o'clock, and the sun was shining, which meant he'd slept through the night and the morning. That was becoming a habit since he'd dropped off Noelle. Had five nights passed already? He needed to pick her up but feared his faculties weren't present enough for him to be the father she deserved.

The dinging continued, followed by pounding on the front door, then a voice. “Thomas, answer your door. I know you’re home.”

Oh, he was going to murder his sister. Certainly, the courts would be lenient on him when they heard his story.

He made it to the door and flung it open. “What is your problem?”

“Nice to see you, too.” She pushed past him as if she owned the place, then stopped. “What in the world?”

He turned and took in the living room and the part of the kitchen visible from the entry.

Oh, boy. Dishes filled the sink. His garbage overflowed with microwave meal trays. Newspapers lay scattered on the couch and coffee table. He’d become a slob.

“I’m sorry.” He closed the door and hurried to the couch, straightened the papers. “Guess I’ve let things go a bit.”

Denise had the nerve to laugh! “You think I’m worried about a newspaper or a few dirty dishes?”

He glanced around, and that was the only thing he saw amiss.

Oh, wait. He ran a hand through hair that needed a trim, not to mention a shampoo. And when was the last time he’d shaved? Though his whiskers still grew at the pace of a twelve-year-old’s beard.

“You are so clueless.” She removed her boots and hung her coat in the closet.

“What?” Dang, there he went again, acting like a

prepubescent boy.

"No wonder your daughter doesn't want to come home."

Now those were fighting words. "What do you want, Denise?"

"Well, I stopped by because I'm tired of hoteling it and figured you had the guest room, but it looks like I should have visited about three weeks ago."

He pinched the bridge of his nose. "Look, I know I'm a clueless male, so can you just spit it out, please?"

"How you succeed as a lawyer, I'll never know." She rolled her eyes, so they were now equal in the childish stage. "Where do you keep your Christmas decorations?" She aimed for the stairs.

"Why do you want . . .?" Oh . . . He looked at the room through newly cleared eyes. It was December, just two days until Christmas, and the living room didn't have as much as a twinkling light up, much less a tree. "In the attic. What's it to you?"

She just shook her head as she stomped up the steps, muttering something he couldn't make out, most likely directed at how obtuse he was. She reached the top of the steps, went to the end of the hallway, and tugged open the always-sticky door leading to the attic, not once checking to see if he followed behind. Which, of course, he did, like always, even though he always grumbled about it.

The Christmas decor sat boxed in plastic containers on a shelf, all labeled so any random person—or Denise—could walk up and easily find what they wanted. She pulled out the box labeled "ornaments" and handed it to him, then she retrieved a container of lights.

Without saying another word, she led him down the two flights of steps into the living room.

He stared at the two containers that were useless without a tree. "We're missing something."

"Oh, no, we're not." She pulled her coat from the closet and handed him a jacket as well.

"What did you do?" He pushed an arm through a sleeve in his coat.

She slipped on her boots. "The correct question is, w*hat did Noelle and I do?*"

"Noelle?" He stopped midway through sleeving the second arm.

"Someone had to take her tree shopping."

He almost retorted, "That's my job," but smartly clamped his mouth shut before he gave her more ammunition to fire at him. Yeah, tree shopping had been his job, but he'd spent the last week sleeping.

Denise strode outside. While putting on his boots, he caught a glimpse of her rental car with a tree on top, but no sign of Noelle. "Did she come with you?"

"She didn't know if you wanted her."

"Of course, I want her."

"You do?" She spun toward him, and he jerked back a step. "Is that why you dropped her off at her grandparents' and left her there? Why you haven't called?"

"I've called." Twice. As an attorney, he'd rip apart that statement.

Her *harumph* succeeded in derailing his lame testimony.

From now on, he was keeping his mouth shut, because anything that came out of it would be a lousy excuse. He helped her remove the tree from the top of the car, and they carried it into the house. They put it into the stand, and he retrieved a level to make certain it wasn't crooked. That, naturally, earned another roll of the eyes.

But she did smile when the tree stood perfectly upright.

He did too as a flicker of life lit inside him.

Together, they sat on the couch, appreciating the Fraser fir that fit perfectly in his living room's bay window nook.

Now it needed ornaments and lights and tinsel.

And presents.

But mostly, it needed Noelle.

"Denise, would you mind giving me a hand with something?"

"I thought that's what I'd been doing?" She nagged, but he could hear the smile in her voice.

"I need to go shopping."

She clapped her hands. "I've been waiting for you to ask." She did love spending his money.

"Then we need to pick up Noelle."

"Now you're talking sense."

Yeah, finally. But before they left, he had one more important phone call to make. He got off the couch and walked to the tree that was empty right now but would soon be decked out with lights and ornaments and tinsel.

More presents than any child deserved would form a mountainous skirt below the tree. Few children would have that. And some had nothing.

Not even a parent to go home to.

He dialed Pastor Jacob, who answered on the first ring as if waiting for Thomas to call.

"Thomas. Good to hear from you. How can I help you?"

He fingered the pine needles, pricking his finger to assure himself he was living for the first time in nearly a month. "Does the Blessing Tree still need volunteers to deliver?"

"As a matter of fact, Thomas, they do."

"Then sign me up."

"Already done, brother, already done. It's what the church body has been praying for." Of course they had, because that was what they did. Pray and serve. And, no doubt, the good pastor had had a one-on-one with God, Who'd told him, *Thomas'll come through.*

He hung up and turned to his older sister, seeing her with a clearer perspective. She might not have the eloquence of an official therapist, but she'd succeeded in breaking through to him where gentle talk had failed to motivate him.

"Why are you staring at me?" She hugged herself as if she were being laid bare.

"Thank you for kicking my butt. It's what I needed. Will still need." He was under no illusion that the peace of this afternoon would last, but he had a sister who loved him enough to not treat him with kid gloves when what he needed was a stern jolt to his behind.

She even grinned. “Just so you know, my foot’s ready and able if—when—you need it.”

“I’m counting on it.”

“You should also know, your entire family has been on their knees for you.”

He knew that too, except . . . “You too?”

“Well, we had a convo.” She glanced upward. “He told me to give my little brother a nudge.”

“I’ll remember to thank Him.”

“Why wait?” She folded her hands and looked down, and for the first time in their lives, brother and sister prayed together.

Chapter Six

Thomas and Noelle walked hand-in-hand into the warehouse used by Blessing Tree to organize gifts before distribution. Christmas Eve was later than they usually distributed, but Pastor Jacob had convinced the organizers that Thomas would come through, long before he knew himself that he'd help. What Thomas would give for that direct-line communication.

Well, really, he already had that direct line to God. Thomas was still working on the listening part.

They entered the room that housed the gifts, and he stopped.

Beside him, Noelle clapped. "I knew it!" Yeah, she had known it, had said as much in her nonstop monologue on the way over.

The tables were empty but for one big, red gift bag. The bag the two of them had filled with gifts for Princess Paris Stockett, which meant one more battle had just been added to this Christmas season.

"Ah, you must be Thomas Nordberg." A large man dressed in Paul Bunyan-like plaid approached from Thomas's right. The man was large enough to be the fabled lumberjack. All he needed was a blue ox to convince a jury.

"I am." Thomas held out his hand and it was engulfed by a massive paw with a tight grip. "And this is my daughter, Noelle."

"Call me William. Nice to meet you both. Pastor Jacob speaks highly of you. Said to make sure we saved this bag for you two to deliver."

"It's the gift we chose!" Noelle bounced at his side.

"It is, now?" William knelt, and he still dwarfed Noelle. "And did you choose the presents?"

"I did, and she's going to love them."

"Aye, I'm sure she will, sweetheart. Shall we pray over it?"

"Can I pray?" Noelle continued her bounce.

"Of course you can."

She reached out her hands to both Thomas and William. "Dear God, thank You for letting us buy presents for Princess Paris. She has the prettiest name! I'm sure it's been tough with her mommy or daddy in jail. Can You help her through it? Just like You helped my daddy 'cause Mommy's in Heaven? And thank You for letting us give them to Princess. I hope she's happy. And thank You, God, for sending Jesus, and for this special Christmas. Amen."

"Amen," Thomas said right along with William.

"That had to be the best prayer I've heard all week." William stood and looked to Thomas. "You have a special child there."

"I do." One that was helping him discover joy amidst their sorrow.

William handed Thomas a slip of paper. "Here's where you deliver. I've just called, and they are home now. There's even a note from her dad. Know you are blessing the girl and her family."

"Yes, we know." Though Thomas still struggled with King Stockett receiving any blessing.

But didn't Jesus forgive that criminal on the cross? One that probably had been justly convicted and deserved to be crucified, unlike Jesus, Who was wrongly accused and found guilty of crimes He didn't commit.

If Jesus on the cross could forgive the criminal, then Thomas could too.

He grasped Noelle's hand and nodded at William. "Thank you for all you do."

"Aw, it's nothing. It's all about letting children know they are loved and not forgotten. That's barely service at all."

He couldn't be more right.

Father and daughter left the warehouse and drove to the address on the sheet of paper, with Noelle jabbering the entire way. It wasn't the best neighborhood in the Boston area, but certainly not the worst. Probably better than what Princess Paris grew up in. What kind of life had King led before he committed the murders? What led him to that place? Had he ever met Jesus?

Had Princess met Jesus?

If not, who better to introduce her to Him than Noelle and him?

He pulled up to the curb of a neatly maintained home. The sidewalk parallel to the street and the one leading to the front door were shoveled right down to the cement, the way he always did it.

Noelle insisted on carrying the bag, heavy as it was, up to the door. She wanted to present it to the girl, and rightly so. The gift was entirely from his daughter's heart.

Thomas pressed the doorbell. An elderly woman with bright, aware eyes answered the door. Just from first appearances, he could tell she was the type of person an attorney loved to have as a witness or a juror.

"May I help you?" she asked.

"This is for Princess Paris," Noelle blurted out before Thomas had time to introduce them.

The woman clapped her hands. "She will be so excited. Won't you come in?"

Noelle peered up at Thomas, seeking permission. A lesson learned from the shopping fiasco.

"Yes, thank you, Ms. . . ."

"Delia James. You may call me Delia."

"And I'm Noelle, because I was born on Christmas Day."

"You were?" Delia clapped her hands again. "What a marvelous gift you were and are."

"She is." Thomas squeezed his daughter's shoulders. "And I'm her father, Thomas Nordberg. Pleased to meet you, Delia."

"Please, come on in. Have a seat." She gestured to the couch. "I'll fetch Princess. She's been quite down, so you will be a welcome sight."

Thomas sat beside his daughter and drew her to his side, giving her a hug. "I'm very proud of you, Chestnut."

"Hello?" A small voice barely registered to Thomas.

"Hi." Noelle leaped off the couch. "Are you Princess Paris?"

The girl nodded, her gaze and her shoulders aimed toward the ground.

"I love your name. It's so pretty."

Though Princess kept her head down, Thomas detected a pinking in her cheeks.

"This is for you." Noelle set the bag in front of the girl. "It's really heavy." Noelle pointed out two cards attached to the bag. "That card's from me and Daddy, and it's for Delia. This one's from your daddy."

"My daddy?" The child finally looked up, and hope filled those sad eyes. "He didn't forget me?"

"Nope. These presents are all from him. He loves you."

A single tear trickled over the child's cheek. She had already shouldered too much in her young life, and to think that Thomas had fought against helping her.

"Yes, Princess Paris." Thomas felt it necessary to reinforce Noelle's words. "He loves you."

"And Jesus loves you, too." Oh, his daughter was going to make a wonderful evangelist. No, actually, she already was winning hearts for Jesus.

"Well." Thomas stood. This unwrapping was meant for

Princess and her new family. "Thank you, Delia, for welcoming us. And it was very nice to meet you, Princess Paris. I hope you both have a blessed Christmas."

He knew it might not be merry, but as he'd learned, a broken and blessed Christmas was undoubtedly better than a merry one anyway. After all, the child Whose birth they would celebrate tomorrow had been crucified thirty-three years after His birth. Without Jesus's body being broken, salvation wasn't possible.

That was cause for joy, and he finally understood Lacy choosing the song "Joy to the World" for the mourners to sing at her life-celebration ceremony.

He walked out of the house with Noelle clinging tightly to his side.

"Thank you, Daddy."

"No, thank you, Noelle, for reminding your daddy Who Christmas is all about. I might still be sad at times."

"I am too, Daddy."

"But you reminded me to think of others in those sad times. You've turned this very broken Christmas into something special. Your mother would be so proud."

"Jesus too?"

"Yes, especially Jesus."

"Weeping may tarry for the night,
but joy comes with the morning."
– Psalm 30:5

Thomas also appears in Brenda S. Anderson's short story, "Hot Cocoa Summers", and in her full-length novel, *Broken Together*.

Note from the Author

The loss of a loved one is always difficult, and grief looks different for each individual. When compounded with a holiday, grief can be especially challenging to navigate. In this story, readers journeyed with Thomas through the five stages of grief: denial, anger, bargaining, depression, and acceptance. Each stage is normal but may not feel so to the person grieving.

Perhaps this story came to me at this time as I'm dealing with a different grieving process. My husband has been diagnosed with early-onset Alzheimer's, so I'm grieving all the losses on this journey, from memories to careers to dreams of growing old together. We've learned it's important to celebrate now and not wait for what tomorrow brings.

God walks with us through our valleys, and joy will come in the morning.

"Joy to the world, our Lord is come!"

~ Brenda

Acknowledgments

Many thanks to Gayle Balster for reading the unedited story and still loving it. Always a "whew!" moment! Thanks to Stacy Monson for helping me spruce up the story and to Lesley Ann McDaniel and Sara Davison for making it shine. To my husband, Marvin, who bears with me during writing seasons.

Before writing each day, I begin with prayer, often saying, "I have no clue what I'm supposed to write today. Help!" And every time God faithfully whispers ideas to me and helps fill in the blank pages. I owe all my stories, all my ideas to Him.

A COMING HOME SERIES NOVELETTE

The Home for Christmas CHALLENGE

BRENDA S. ANDERSON

THE HOME FOR CHRISTMAS CHALLENGE

A Coming Home Series Novelette

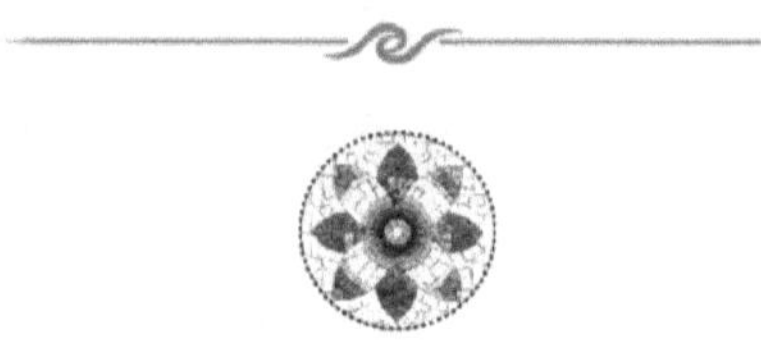

Christmas isn't Christmas without drama,
and this season might be the worst of all.

Dating hasn't been on Lee Aldrich's mind since Amelia's mother abandoned the two of them over thirteen years ago. Since it's the last year before his daughter heads off to college, he wants to make the upcoming holiday season memorable. Unfortunately, Amelia has other plans, beginning with a blind date for Lee. A date that stirs up memories of the past that he has no desire to revisit.

But if Lee wants to have Christmas with his daughter, he and his date need to accept Amelia's Home for Christmas Challenge. As the months pass, Christmas nears, and the challenges continue, forcing Lee to face hard truths. If he doesn't meet the truth head on, he risks losing what he cherishes the most.

This story originally appeared in The Mosaic Collection's 2023 Christmas anthology, *A Thrill in the Air*.

"Therefore, confess your sins to one another and pray for one another, that you may be healed. The prayer of a righteous person has great power as it is working."
James 5:16

Chapter One

The father-daughter roles had been flipped on their head.

Lee Aldrich chuckled as he examined the clothes arranged neatly on his bed. A decade ago he'd done the same for Amelia for her first years of school. Now she was caring for him, although he wasn't terribly happy with the reason.

What kind of daughter sets their dad up on a blind date?

Apparently, his.

He dressed in the outfit Amelia had picked out for him during their excruciating afternoon of shopping. He would rather stick his finger in a live socket than go through that torture again.

The date tonight was going to be a different kind of torture. He didn't need a woman to fulfill him, hadn't since Elise had walked out on him thirteen years ago. But he'd do anything to please his daughter, even go on a lousy blind date.

A knock sounded on his bedroom door.

"Come in," he said, knowing it would be Amelia.

She breezed inside the room and her gaze traveled from his black captain shoes to his new jeans, a blue button-down shirt, and then his hair she'd styled like Chris Evans's. Or so she claimed. Hey, if it was good enough for Captain America . . .

"You approve?" He crossed his arms, uncomfortable with the scrutiny.

She scrunched her lips and waved a finger, indicating she wanted him to turn around.

With a loud sigh, he obeyed, then turned back and splayed his arms. "If this isn't good enough, we can always call off the evening."

"Don't you wish." Finally, she grinned. "You look passable."

"Gee thanks."

"No, seriously, you look amazing. Who knew an electrician could clean up so nice?"

"Why do I feel like I'm being insulted?" With a grunt, he grabbed his wallet and phone off of his dresser and stuffed them in his back pockets.

"Sorry, that's not what I meant. You look fabulous. No qualifiers." She wrapped an arm in his and led him out to the living room, where she straightened his collar. "Promise you won't be home before ten."

"Ten oh one it is, then." That would be nearly two hours with a stranger. Wasn't that long enough?

At least Amelia had chosen Lee's favorite steak

restaurant in Brainerd, one that wouldn't be too loud to hear each other. Hopefully, this woman could hold up her end in a conversation.

"Fine." She gestured toward the door leading to the garage. "Time to go, or you'll be late and set a bad first impression."

"I'm going." He raised his hands in surrender and aimed for the garage. "What's her name again?" He grinned as he listened for her response.

"Nuh-uh. I know you. I give you her name, and you're doing a google search to learn all about her and ruin the surprise. All you need to know is that you're perfect for each other. Her daughter agrees."

Lee had no response to that as he escaped the house and climbed into his pickup. He backed out of the garage and onto a quiet Granite Creek street that had changed little since his once-intact family moved there over thirteen years ago.

After all these years, why did Amelia need him to date now? At the beginning of his single parenthood, he'd longed for a helpmeet, a woman who would be a mom to Amelia, yet they'd survived the pre-teen and now most of the teen years with barely a hiccup.

All he knew was that he had no desire to date. Over the next year, he had one goal, and that was to make it a memorable year for him and Amelia before she left him for college. How could his daughter be old enough for college already? Wasn't she born just a year or two ago?

Work had gotten in the way too often, but raising a

daughter while running your own electric business wasn't easy, even if Amelia spent half her weekends and holidays with her mother. This year, though . . . this year was for Amelia. Not for his customers, and certainly not for some stranger Amelia wanted him to meet.

He pulled onto the Minnesota state highway that was less crowded since Labor Day had just passed, and all the cabin owners had closed up for the season. He headed toward Brainerd and his date. If Amelia wanted him to meet someone, he'd appease her. He'd even try to be on his best behavior. Chances were, this woman was as thrilled to meet him as he was to meet her. He'd behave like a gentleman and treat a woman as she deserved, even if it was just one evening.

In his rearview mirror, he watched the sun edge toward the horizon, a beautiful way to cap off this early September day, and a reminder that God was still in charge. Something he'd come to believe after his family fell apart.

He drummed his fingers on the steering wheel. What attitude would God want him to have tonight, beyond treating this woman as a precious child of God?

"You're going to have to help me with that." With a smirk, he briefly looked up.

The miles passed, the town drew near, and butterflies took flight in his gut. He was nervous? Didn't that mean he wanted to make a good impression, that maybe getting to know someone was a good idea? Life had to be more than working, and when Amelia left for college in a year, he'd be alone.

Alone. He gulped at the idea. Yeah, Amelia was right about this. A slow smile crept to his face. If tonight didn't work out, maybe he'd start putting himself out there, sign up for one of those online dating services. He laughed at that. Nah, technological dating wasn't for him. All that mattered was that he enjoyed the evening.

At last, the restaurant came into view, nestled among woods that surrounded one of the many lakes in the area. His stomach growled in anticipation of the steak.

He parked his pickup and glanced in the rearview mirror to check his hair. Dang, he was nervous. He climbed out, smoothed wrinkles on his shirt, then made his way inside.

The host, dressed mostly in black, greeted him with a smile. "Good evening, do you have reservations?"

"I do." He gave his name. "I'm meeting someone and requested the corner booth with the lake view." That was what Amelia had told him anyway.

"Of course." She made a mark on the tablet in front of her and grabbed a menu. "Right this way."

Lee followed her through the dimly lit room filled with patrons speaking in hushed tones. A perfect setting for a date. They'd be able to talk and be heard. The scent of steak wafted toward him, and his stomach growled. Regardless of how the date went, he'd be happy to have a good piece of meat.

Someone already sat in the booth the host directed him to, with their back to him. Wavy blond locks that fell to narrow shoulders and slender arms, hands that already held a menu. This was a good start.

But what he'd give for some water right now, to calm nerves jumping as bad as a school kids'. "I will have a good night tonight," he whispered to himself to calm the jitters. If something came of the evening, he'd thank his daughter. And if it turned out to be a dud, maybe he'd let Amelia set him up again. Or maybe not.

Elise Kraemer tapped her manicured fingers on the table while staring out the window at Gull Lake brimming with boats, pontoons, and jet skis. Why she'd bothered with a manicure for a stranger, she didn't know. It wasn't as if she'd ever had difficulty attracting men, and not a one had cared about her fingernails.

They'd been more allured by her medical degree and her bank account, which had taught her to give up on the dating life.

But she'd do anything for Amelia.

"Hello, I'm supposed to—"

Her eyes widened as she turned toward the too-familiar voice, and her mouth hung open.

Oh, Amelia was in big trouble.

"Well." She cleared her throat and regained her voice. "If it isn't Leopold Aldrich?" Her ex. And her daughter's father.

Smirking, she gestured to the seat across from her. Their little sneak of a daughter was going to be grounded for life.

He crossed his arms and glowered down at her. “This was a mistake.”

“Oh, no it wasn’t.” Amelia’s voice came from behind Lee. Elise had been so focused on the man hovering above her, she hadn’t noticed Amelia sneak up behind him.

Lee spun toward their daughter, his jaw tight. That informed Elise he was holding back a good tongue lashing.

“Uh-uh.” Amelia wagged her finger and nodded toward the booth. “This is where you put on your big boy pants and sit down.”

Elise chuckled. Their daughter had inherited Elise’s temperament, that was for certain. She covered her mouth to hide her grin, even though she actually agreed with Lee that this—whatever *this* was—was a mistake.

He sat, that glower taking over his still-handsome face. No doubt, he was cooking up some punishment for when the two arrived home. Good thing for Amelia that tonight was Lee’s night with her because the punishment Elise would dole out wouldn’t be as charitable as his.

Elise scooted over for Amelia to sit, but she pulled up a chair and sat at the table’s end instead.

“I won’t be long.” Amelia opened her massive purse, removed two notebooks, and handed one to her and the other to Lee. On the front of each, someone had scribbled “Home for Christmas Challenge.” Perhaps written by one of the children Amelia babysat. “Since I plan to become a teacher, I figured now is a good time to start practicing giving out homework.”

Uh-oh. Elise opened the book—a journal, actually—to the first page. Amelia had written, "Find Your Center" at the top in all caps.

"What do you mean by this?" Lee practically took the words out of Elise's mouth.

"What do you think it means?" Amelia rested her elbows on the table and her chin on her folded hands.

The impertinent child. Oh, she was too much like her mother.

Elise paged through the rest of the journal. All blank.

"Sounds like some new age gobbledy-gook, if you ask me." Lee closed the notebook.

"You know me better than that." She took Lee's journal and wrote *Matthew 6:33* below the title. "There. That's the only hint the two of you are getting."

Oh, their child looked awfully smug sitting there, her arms crossed.

"When and where do we turn in this homework?" Lee grumbled like he'd done back in high school over any assignment. He liked problems with numbers and hard facts that to him were easily solved, not something vague.

"You have until this Thursday."

Elise opened the calendar on her phone, and Lee did the same.

"Oh, you're both free. I already added it to your schedules."

"What?" Lee jabbed at his phone. "You hacked my phone?"

"Well, it does sync with that co-parenting app you guys

are signed up for."

"Oh," Lee mumbled.

Elise just stared at the entry on her phone. *Homework assignment #1 due* was highlighted in bright blue. Under *Location*, the calendar read *Paul Bunyan State Trail, Picnic Shelter*.

"And if we don't do the homework?" Lee beat her to the question.

Amelia pulled out her phone and tapped at it. "As you know, my eighteenth birthday is coming soon."

Elise knew that all too well. Her spirited daughter was about to leave her an empty nester, which was why she'd agreed to this so-called date in the first place. Even though Amelia spent much more time at Lee's, her too-large house was going to feel awfully empty.

"What does your birthday have to do with this?" Elise waved her hand over the notebook and gestured to Lee. "With us?"

Amelia sat back in her chair, her sassy demeanor suddenly replaced with a flatlined mouth and dark eyes. "Katie is spending Christmas vacation with her aunt and uncle in New York, and she's invited me to go with her."

Elise glanced at her calendar again. Winter break began a day before Amelia turned eighteen, which was nine days before Christmas, and ended January second. Her daughter couldn't mean the entire vacation, could she? She studied her daughter's face then dared look across at Lee. Clearly, he'd drawn the same conclusion, that their daughter was blackmailing them.

Lee laid down his phone and ran a hand down his face that held a perpetual frown, then stared at their daughter. “What about Christmas at Aunt Lydia’s? We’ve been planning that week at the ranch for over a year?”

“I guess that depends upon you,” Amelia said, her face expressionless.

“Okay, then. What’s your goal?” Such a Lee question. “Because if it’s that you want the two of us back together . . .”

“Would that be so bad?” A tear hovered beneath Amelia’s eye, and she blinked it away.

Oh, yes it would. “Sweetheart.” Elise slid from her seat and wrapped Amelia in a hug. “No matter what you bribe us with, your father and I aren’t getting back together.”

Amelia shrugged out of Elise’s hug. She raised her chin and stood. “That’s your choice. But also know, on my next birthday I’ll be an adult, so I can make my own choices as well.”

Their daughter spun and stalked from the restaurant, drawing stares from other diners.

Well, this was a mess. Elise slunk onto the bench and bowed her head. The air seemed to close in around her, stealing her breath. They couldn’t miss Amelia’s birthday or her last Christmas at home before going off to college, but her demands were too high. No way could Elise or Lee afford paying them.

Which meant she’d spend the rest of the evening on her knees, beseeching God for a solution. She grabbed her clutch and began to slide from the bench.

Lee's phone pinged, and his frown deepened.

"Is there another problem?" Elise hovered on the edge, wanting to leave, but her gut—or was it her conscience?—told her to stay.

Lee chuckled. Shook his head. "I'd promised her I wouldn't be home before ten, which means I have an hour and a half to kill."

"Sorry about that." Just because Lee had to stay late, didn't mean she had to. She needed to get outside where she could breathe again. "Enjoy your steak."

"Yeah, there is that. The night won't be a total waste."

"I guess not." Elise serpentined around the tables and out of the restaurant, where she finally filled her lungs with fresh air. She'd meant it when she said they couldn't get back together, not when it was her fault that they'd broken up in the first place.

Chapter Two

What a mess.

Lee picked up the menu and reminded himself of the words he'd thought when entering tonight. If the date was a dud, at least he'd have steak.

Tonight hadn't been a dud, though. It had been an implosion.

How could Amelia begin to think that he and Elise would get back together? His heart hadn't recovered from what she'd done to him thirteen years ago. Probably never would.

He glanced at the menu, his gaze scrolling down until he found what his watering mouth wanted: the filet mignon with buttery mashed potatoes and the chef's choice of veggie. Yeah, it was pricy, but after what Amelia had just put him through, it was worth the cost. He might even have an adult beverage to go with it. He'd planned on ordering wine with his date, but he'd settle for a beer.

He studied the beverage menu. Elise would have liked

the cabernet sauvignon from Geyser Peak in California. Berry, chocolate, and smooth.

"Am I driving you to drink?"

Startled by Elise's voice, he dropped the menu and was struck mute as she slid in across from him.

"Let me see what they have." She took the menu from him and scanned it as if everything was natural rather than upside down and inside out.

"What are you—"

"That cabernet sauvignon from Geyser Peak sounds divine." She set down the drink menu and reached for the one with food. "What do you recommend? I'm assuming it's still a favorite place."

"Time-out here." He gave the time-out signal with his hands. "I thought you were leaving. I was going to enjoy a steak in silence."

She just shrugged. "I felt sorry for you. What can I say?"

"That you'll leave?" *Please?*

"Sorry. I think that promise you made to Amelia was for both of us." She set the menu down and smiled at him in a way that made his gut churn. "I can't be the reason you didn't keep it."

"Like you've kept your commitments in the past?"

She blinked and nodded. "Touché."

He sighed. That was a low blow that the Lee from thirteen years ago would have delivered, not the new, redeemed Lee. "Sorry."

"It's the truth." She shrugged as if he hadn't hurt her, but her silence and her intense focus on the menu indicated he'd hit her right where he'd been aiming.

"I hear their salmon is amazing," Lee said. Talking food worked as an apology, didn't it?

She flipped the menu closed. "Then salmon it is." She raised her gaze to his. "It's true that I came back because Amelia would have wanted it."

"Yes, but—"

"But, we didn't listen closely."

"Are you ready to order?" Somehow the waitress had snuck up to the table without his noticing. They both ordered, and Lee informed the server to put it all on one bill, in spite of Elise's protests. Call him old fashioned, but he still believed a guy should pay for his date. Once upon a time, Elise had appreciated that, until her profession had changed her.

After the server left, Elise leaned toward him, resuming where they'd left off. "Our assignment isn't to get back together, even if that's what she ultimately wants, but it's simply to do the assignments."

"That sounds deceptive." And he wouldn't lie to Amelia.

"Not if we're up front with our intentions."

He considered that. If they told Amelia up front, which they already had, that there would be no reconciliation, that wouldn't be deceptive. Elise's plan could work.

"Okay, then." Lee flipped open the notebook and read out loud. "Find your center, Matthew 6:33." For the life of him, he couldn't memorize scripture. He opened his Bible app to look it up.

"That one's easy." Elise raised her brows in that way of hers that told others she was superior. "'But seek first the kingdom of God and his righteousness, and all these things will be added to you.'"

Startled, gaped at Elise. She didn't have her phone out to search for the verse. "You know that one?"

"You'd be surprised at what I know."

"I'm surprised you even read the Bible."

She patted her heart. "Another well-aimed shot."

Oh, man, he was being an idiot, but seriously, when they had been together, her focus was all about science, and God's being a crutch or proof of people's low intelligence. Still, he felt like sinking into the floor. If only they still had the menu, so he could distract himself.

"You really didn't know?"

He forced his gaze to Elise and shook his head.

"Two years ago." Her face lit up with a genuine smile, with eyes that shone. "I realized that God and science weren't mutually exclusive, but rather the opposite. Your daughter had something to do with that. She's quite the evangelist."

"Tell me about it." Although his conversion had taken place shortly after Elise left him and Amelia, thanks to Katie, Amelia's best friend then and now. His faith in Christ was the only thing that got him through those first years of being a single dad.

To a child that both he and Elise loved. They could put aside their differences for a few months, couldn't they? After all, they'd once been best friends. It wouldn't hurt either of them to get along for Amelia's sake.

He tapped the notebook. "You game?"

Elise showed a half smile. "Anything to keep our daughter home for Christmas." Her smile grew to a grin. "Even if it means spending time with you."

"Then Thursday is a date."

"No." She shook her head, a bit too vehemently, in his opinion. "Not a date. But I'll see you at the park."

Lee peddled hard for the last mile of the Paul Bunyan Trail, the reds, oranges, and yellows of fall exploding around him. Reminded him of when he'd first met Elise back in grade school. He was biking with his family, and his little sister lost her balance and fell. Elise happened to be biking toward them and saw the mishap. She was only eight-years-old at the time, yet she'd braked and hurried to help Lydia. She'd pulled a small first aid kit from her fanny pack and taken care of the scrape.

Even as a nine-year-old, Lee had been impressed. Had his first crush. After that, Lee and Elise had been inseparable.

Until she'd cleaved them apart with the precision of a surgeon.

Affairs will do that to a couple.

He shook off that thought and banished the anger that frequently made its appearance at the thought of Elise.

Which was why this Home for Christmas Challenge

made him more nervous than the blind date had. That evening had ended okay. They'd managed to play nice, enjoy their meals, and talk mostly about their daughter. He'd even held his tongue when Elise had left herself wide open for criticism. That meant he was growing, right?

Or did it mean he had a whole bunch of room to grow yet?

Probably a little of both.

Regardless, spending any time with someone he'd learned to despise wasn't something he looked forward to, but he'd made the sacrifice for Amelia.

He arrived at the shelter ten minutes prior to their scheduled time, and was pleased to see that it was empty. That would give him time to prepare spiritually. After all, considering Amelia's assignment, that was what this evening was about.

He dismounted his bike, tugged off his helmet, and steered into the shelter that overlooked the Mississippi. He parked his bike beside a picnic table and removed Amelia's notebook from his backpack.

Beneath the words *Find Your Center* and the Bible verse from Matthew 6:33, he'd drawn a circle and placed a cross in the middle. After that, he'd poured out tough truths. Too often he was his own center, or Amelia, or his work. They all took the place where God belonged. The fact that his daughter made this part of his assignment, meant that she could easily see his focus was off.

He'd already initiated making the changes in his life. Praying and reading the Bible the first thing every morning. Hold conversations with God throughout the day. Bring everything—his praises and his problems—to God and lay them at His feet. For someone who liked to be in control, that was difficult, but necessary.

No doubt, Elise was struggling with the same issues.

On his phone, he opened his Bible app to Luke 10. He now began his day with Proverbs and ended with the Psalms. This year, he was working his way through the rest of the Bible chronologically. Sandwiching the daily reading with Psalms and Proverbs had given him a new perspective.

Reading about Martha and her need for control and gave him a different perspective of himself.

"Hey there."

Lee pulled his attention from his phone and looked back at Amelia. He patted the bench beside himself. "How was school?"

She shrugged. "Just school. When I'm a teacher, I'm going to make it interesting."

"I'm sure you will." Lee gave his daughter a hug, then glanced at the clock on his phone. Ten minutes after six already. For the ultra-precise Elise, that was unconscionably late. "Any sign of your mom yet?"

"No." Amelia checked her phone, and worry drew her brows together. "And no message either. She told me she wasn't on call, so that shouldn't be a problem, and even when she is called in, she always lets me know."

"I'm sure it's nothing." He held up the notebook. "But this sure wasn't." Then he attempted to distract Amelia by talking about what he'd learned this week, but couldn't help noticing her frequent looks back and peeking at her phone.

To be honest, when his phone showed six thirty, concern nagged at him as well. "You don't suppose she stood us up, do you?"

"I thought of that." Amelia worried her lower lip. "But she messaged me this morning. Said she'd be here."

"Do you have a tracker on your phone?" Amelia was able to track his whereabouts and he hers.

"Ha! When I told Mom you'd let me follow you, she laughed."

"Has she ever done this before? Just not shown up for something?"

"Never. Not without letting me know."

"Maybe she went to the wrong picnic shelter. This isn't the only one."

"I sent her the map earlier, just like I did you. She said she knows right where it is."

He took his daughter's hand. "I'm sure it's nothing, but let's pray."

Amelia nodded.

Lee looked out over the mighty river as he brought Elise to God. "You know where she is, Lord. Protect her and strengthen our faith to trust in You." They continued praying for several more minutes as the sun crept down the horizon. Time ticked past, and full-blown worry now ate at his gut.

He couldn't sit and wait any longer. "Let's head over to

her place." He didn't know what he expected to find, but he couldn't sit here and do nothing.

"I don't want to drive." Her voice trembled.

"That's okay. We'll take my pickup and get your car later."

With one arm around Amelia's shoulder, and one hand balancing his bike, he hurried to the parking lot. He secured his bike in the truck bed then hopped in the cab and hit the ignition button just as Amelia's phone sang.

"It's Mom!" She stabbed at the phone and answered. "Where are you?"

Lee heard mumbling on the other end of the phone, but couldn't make it out. "Can you put her on speaker?"

Amelia hit the speaker button. "Dad's listening now. Could you repeat?"

"Sorry I'm not there." Her voice was still shrouded by what sounded like heavy traffic. Had she been in an accident? That was what had continuously crossed Lee's mind.

"A bear ran out in—"

"You were hit by a bear?" Lee turned off the pickup, so he could hear better.

She sighed dramatically, a trait he remembered too well. "If you'd listen, you'd hear the story."

"Fine. Zipping my lips."

"The car in front of me hit a bear. I had to stop and make sure everyone was okay."

Oh. Of course she had to. He wouldn't expect anything else.

"And calling you wasn't on my mind."

Amelie sniffled. "We were so worried."

"We?" Elise said with a happy lilt. "You do care, Lee."

He snorted, but couldn't come up with a clever retort, so instead he said, "So, you're okay? What about the people in the car?"

"What about the bear?" Naturally, Amelia worried about the animal.

"The family is okay. Just superficial injuries. Nothing that requires hospitalization or surgery, but I did recommend they get checked out at the hospital."

"What about the bear?" Amelie's voice grew insistent.

"I'm sorry, hon. He ran off and the authorities are searching for him. But I'm afraid his injuries will be too severe."

Lee wasn't surprised to see the trail of tears roll down Amelia's cheeks. If he'd been telling the story, he'd have left that last part off.

"Do you mind if I beg off for the night, though, sweetheart? I'm used to dealing with injuries, but not witnessing what brought them about, and I'm exhausted."

Amelia wiped at her eyes. "That's okay, if you can just tell us what you learned. Dad learned he has to stop putting himself at the center. That he needs to put God there instead."

Elise laughed. "Your father and I are too much alike in that respect."

Wasn't that the truth?

"I'm working on seeking God first. Was even praying as

I was driving, and that's when I saw the accident. I know He put me here at this specific time."

"Then you both get A's on your first assignment."

Lee flexed his arm. "Of course, I did."

"Yeah, don't go getting a big head, Leopold."

He chuckled at the name that always humbled him, especially when Elise used it.

"This next assignment should be an easy one, but it's super important." Amelia pressed and swiped at her phone. "The next class is scheduled for three weeks from now, Friday. It's on both of your calendars. You'll find the details there."

"Very good." An engine roared on Elise's end. Showing off the power of her BMW, no doubt. "I'll be there." Elise's phone went silent.

Abrupt. Typical.

"You good driving home, kiddo?"

"Sure." She opened the door and slid out. "See you at home."

He watched her go to her shiny red Mazda coupe that Elise had spoiled her with when Amelia passed her driver's test. At least, Lee didn't have to pay the insurance. Amelia drove off, then Lee opened the family app schedule and looked up the next assignment. A Friday night football game at the high school. That wouldn't be too awful. The crowd would be too loud for them to have any conversation. He could just enjoy the game.

Then he read the assignment. "You've found your Center. Yay! Now it's time to add to your team (think football). Bring their names and positions to the game and be prepared to tell me why you chose them. Also, bring your phone records to prove you've been in contact with them. Go Team Lee!"

Lee placed his phone in the center console and stared straight ahead into a night sky that had grown dark, save for the first twinkles of stars. A light shot through the sky. A shooting star? Was that a sign of some kind?

Who knew? What he did know was that Amelia was wrong. This next assignment wasn't an easy one. Over the years he'd become a loner, with all his efforts going to Amelia and his career. He didn't have a team, and clearly his very wise daughter knew that.

Chapter Three

Elise strode toward the ticket booth, trying to recall the last time she'd attended a high school football game. Probably twenty-seven years ago during her senior year of high school. She and Lee had attended every game from that first one of their sophomore year when their relationship took a turn.

She almost blushed thinking about those-young-and-in-love days. Part of her would love to recapture that feeling again. Just not with Lee.

"Mom." Amelia jogged toward her, with Katie and her younger sister lagging behind.

Interesting to see those two here. They attended the same small-town school that Amelia did. Choosing a school had resulted in many an argument between Elise and Lee. She wanted Amelia to attend the private school in Brainerd. Lee wanted her in the Granite Creek school system where his friend, and Katie's dad, was the principal.

Lee had eventually won that argument, mostly because he was the one who would have to drive Amelia to school. For years, Elise had held a grudge, but only recently had she admitted Lee's choice was best.

Oh, she'd hated Lee winning at anything. How very selfish she'd been. About so much more than school.

"Mom!" Amelia waved a piece of paper in Elise's face. "You daydreaming or something?"

Elise shook her head. "Or something." She smiled at Katie and Lilly who'd finally caught up. "I'm surprised to see you two here tonight."

"Katie has a boyfriend," Lilly said in a singsong tone, her entire face lighting up with her grin.

Katie looked down but not before Elise caught her blush. "He's playing tonight."

"How fun. I hope you girls enjoy your evening. Tell your parents hello."

"I will!" Lilly bounded away, and Katie sighed. "I'm going to be spending more time watching her than the game."

Oh, the challenges a child with Down syndrome brought. Elise had seen it often in her work with pediatrics, but Katie handled it well, and Lilly was a big part of Amelia's decision to become a special ed teacher. Which made Elise and Lee proud.

Speaking of Lee . . . she sighed. It was time to get her ticket and find him. She aimed for the ticket booth again.

"Mo-om." Agitation rang in Amelia's voice as she waved the paper in Elise's face again. "I have your ticket already."

"Oh, that's what that is. How nice of you to buy a ticket for me."

"Not from me, silly. Dad bought it. He said it was tradition."

Elise stilled, nodded. Other things were tradition, too. "I believe I know where he's sitting."

She hurried away from her daughter, toward the entrance. They'd always sat in the same spot in the bleachers. He'd treated her to whatever food she wanted. He'd been old fashioned in that way. Once upon a time, she'd appreciated that in his character, until her ego had gotten in the way.

She shoved that thought away as she entered the stadium and hung a right. Too often, she beat herself up, but her team—the one she'd organized, thanks to Amelia—was helping her to get over that, to see that she was redeemed and beloved, even with all her baggage.

She kept her gaze forward as she walked past three sets of steps, then took the last set up to the top to the far end of the bleachers.

Their spot.

Lee was there, of course, with the homework notebook on his lap. Hers was in her tote bag that she set at her feet. He handed her a bag of popcorn. "Can't break with tradition."

No, no they couldn't. Without saying anything, she sat, keeping an Amelia-sized space between them. This was too familiar, and it made her heart pump to a wacky beat that no patient monitor could follow.

"Are you okay?" Lee asked with his mouth full, a habit he still hadn't broken. It still irritated her.

"I'm fine," she said in a clipped manner.

"I can tell."

With that tone, she could almost see him roll his eyes.

"I'm sorry," they both said at the same time.

And she glanced his way. "That was uncalled for. I'm just trying to work through this homework Amelia has us doing."

"And the locations."

"Yes, that. The supper club you took me to on our first date."

"That didn't even cross my mind that night, but I did think about meeting you on that bike path where you stopped to help my sister."

"How is Lydia doing, by the way?"

He grinned. "Happy as can be with her five kids and cowboy husband in Wyoming."

"I never pictured her to be a rancher."

"Me neither, but God had other plans."

Yes, He did. "And now there's here." Elise looked out over the stadium filling up with blue and white. She'd intentionally chosen a blue sweatshirt for the night to match. As did Lee. As they always had since that very first game, sitting in this very spot where they'd shared their first kiss and their relationship had crossed over from best friends as naturally as night giving way to day.

"What happened to us, Elise?"

She felt his intense gaze on her, but refused to turn his

way, refused to reply when he full well knew the answer.

"Things were off long before . . ." He shrugged. "Well, you know."

The affair. He never could name it, as if saying it aloud made her deceit more painful. Now, that once gorgeous cardiac surgeon she'd thrown her relationship with Lee away for, had a keg-sized belly and not a lick of hair, while Lee . . .

She stole a quick glance at the man beside her. Strands of gray colored the hair by his temple, and his hairline might be receding a bit, but that didn't detract from his look. Actually, it made him very attractive. He'd never had a six-pack but had always kept himself in shape. Still did. It was a wonder no woman had snatched him up since their breakup.

But Lee was right about the affair. That had been the tip of their melting iceberg. "Do you think if we'd gotten married, things would have turned out differently? I know I wouldn't have found it as easy to leave."

He shrugged. "I've thought about that but doubt it would have saved us."

"I've learned only Jesus can do that."

His eyes connected with hers and that familiar feeling of butterflies taking flight awakened in her belly. As much as she wanted to turn away, she couldn't, and for the life of her, she couldn't shake the desire of wanting him to kiss her like he had the first night here and then every Friday football game thereafter.

"Hey, Lee and Elise. Still in your ol' make-out spot, I see."

Elise tore her gaze from Lee and looked back. Squinted. "Benji?"

The rotund man laughed. "I go by Ben now, but yeah. How you two doing? Haven't seen you for forever."

Lee stood and shook the man's beefy hand. "We're well. And you?"

She appreciated that Lee didn't go into their sordid history. A stranger didn't need to know the details.

"Well, Hannah and I got married, had a couple kids. First grandkid is on the way. Life's treated us well."

"That's good to hear." Lee looked beyond the man's shoulder. "And here comes our daughter, Amelia."

The man turned and nodded. "Nice to meet you, young lady. Your folks used to steam up the bleachers here, back in the day."

Oh brother.

Amelia's face turned a bright red. Time to say goodbye to Benji before he embarrassed them further.

She forced a smile and held out her hand. "It was good seeing you again. You'll have to greet Hannah for us."

"I'll do that. Too bad she's not here. She'd love to see you both. Enjoy the game. Go Warriors!"

"Go Warriors," Lee repeated with half the enthusiasm, as the man bounded down the bleacher steps, shaking the seats as he went.

Then Amelia glanced between them. "Seriously? What if I came here with my boyfriend and made out?"

"Boyfriend?" Elise's eyes went wide and she plopped down on the bench.

"Fictitious boyfriend, okay, but geez, you two were that couple? You just said you shared your first kiss here."

Elise felt her own face grow red. "Well, that and a few other . . ." Elise cleared her throat. ". . . kisses." Her daughter didn't need to know all the details.

"Oh brother." Amelia rolled her eyes as only a teenaged girl can do, then she pointed to the now narrow gap between Lee and Elise. "Mind if I squeeze in here? Nice to see you two getting along."

Elise scooted over. If only Amelia knew how very well she and Lee had been getting along before Benji came along and ruined their moment, she might have stayed away. Elise didn't know whether she should be angry at the man or thankful.

Music blasted through the loudspeakers and a voice boomed over that, announcing the home team as the players ran onto the field, flanked by the cheer team. Cheers erupted from the crowd and the bleachers began filling in. The announcer welcomed the visiting team, who were greeted with boos.

From there on in, talking would be futile. Guess that was why she and Lee had spent the game making out. She smiled at the memory, but if they ever caught Amelia behaving that way? She'd be grounded until the end of the school year.

Oh, the two of them had done so many things wrong. It was a wonder they'd lasted at all. Nothing that broken could be fixed, could it?

Amelia pointed to Elise's tote bag and practically

yelled, "Got your homework?"

Elise nodded and pulled out her notebook, then handed it to her daughter. She'd established a team, though it hadn't been easy, not when so many of her relationships with men and women were superficial.

Elise had spoken with Luella--a woman at church, whom she'd long admired--about being Elise's mentor. Luella had eagerly said yes and had taken her role to heart by connecting with Elise every few days. Then there was the Gloria, the new nurse in the NICU section of the hospital who was always praying for the babies. She had gladly agreed to be a prayer warrior. The last one had been tough. She wanted a mom who would be willing to speak difficult truths to Elise, and finally asked Katie's mom—who happened to be a marriage and family counselor. Debbie said she'd be honored to be the truth teller on Elise's team.

Amelia studied both notebooks as the game got underway. After a few minutes, she placed the open books side by side and pointed to two names: Debbie and Jerry. Katie's parents. Then her finger underlined the name, Marcus, the man who'd given Lee a job after Elise left him. He also happened to be Katie's uncle.

That young woman and her family sure had made an impact on Elise's broken family's life.

Amelia found a marker in her own bag and drew a big A+ on each page as the crowd cheered during a long run play.

Lee grinned, and Elise felt pretty proud herself. Before

they knew it, this challenge would be done, and life would go back to the way it was before, without the Lee distraction.

That shouldn't make her sad, but it did.

Her phone pinged, and apparently, Lee's did as well, and they each awoke their phones. A text from Amelia. Well, that was one way to communicate in the middle of a crowd.

It read:

Your next class session is scheduled for November 1. Check the date for your assignment.

Elise quickly opened the calendar and scrolled to November. She read the assignment, and her heart dropped. It fell even further when she read the location: Cameron Park in Bemidji. The place where Lee had gotten down on one knee and asked her to move in with him. She'd found it romantic, and believed that living together made much more sense than wasting money on a wedding.

Of all the mistakes the two of them had made, that was probably the worst, and was the beginning of their downfall.

Now she'd have to face that dreadful moment once again.

Even as cheers filled the stadium following a touchdown by the home team, Lee felt sick as he read the instructions for their next assignment. It was bad enough that Amelia wanted them to meet at the place where he'd made such a stupid decision. They easily could have gone to a justice of the peace to get married, but no, they were modern and didn't need that license.

And they'd had no faith to ground or inform them.

What was worse, though, was the homework. It was titled "What I Did Wrong" with specific instructions to be honest about his part in the breakup. He'd never faced that truth before and wasn't sure he could bear it now. But he'd do whatever he had to keep his daughter home for Christmas, even if it meant he learned that he was just as responsible for tearing up their family as Elise was.

Chapter Four

It was his fault.

Lee gazed out the window of his pickup at Cameron Park. Typical for November first, temps in the thirties with light snowflakes. Elise and Amelia had stayed the previous night at a hotel because she had a feeling she wouldn't want to drive home.

Snowflakes gathered on his front window, beginning to block his view of the park. With temperatures playing yo-yo with the freezing mark, he'd stay in the warm truck until Elise and Amelia arrived.

How was he going to tell her what he'd realized? That had been his prayer these past weeks. His team members' prayer as well. God sure had a way of shining the light on truth. Why did it have to be so painful?

He prayed still as he waited for Elise to arrive with Amelia. Hopefully, those two were enjoying their weekend in Bemidji. Their relationship had changed over the last months. They'd both matured, it seemed, and part of him envied their closeness, but mostly he was glad for Amelia to have the mother-daughter relationship she'd long desired. He prayed over them and this afternoon, that God would use all of them in a mighty way.

Elise laughed at Amelia's joke as they turned into the parking lot at Cameron Park. The levity sure helped prepare her for this coming "class" with Lee. She wasn't sure what Amelia expected, but she'd find out soon. What she did know was that her daughter would make a great counselor. These exercises the past couple of months had helped clear so much baggage from her mind and heart. She hadn't felt this light or free since high school.

And now witnessing the maturity of her daughter, there'd been a shift in their relationship. Still mother-daughter, but more now. In Amelia, she now had a confidant, not in all things, but in those that mattered, and Elise thanked God for this gift.

Lee's truck was the only one in the parking lot, not a surprise with the frigid weather Bemidji anticipated today. His head was bowed. Praying, likely. Funny how a few years ago she'd regarded that as a weakness, and now she admired the strength it gave him.

Speaking of shifting relationships, something had changed between her and Lee. The animosity was gone and, to be honest, that old attraction was there. She didn't know what to make of it. But that was okay, her team had assured her. Just let God keep leading, and things would work out His way.

But, oh, giving over control was difficult.

She parked beside the pickup, and Lee's head bobbed up. He gave a small smile. A wave. Then he stepped out of his truck, pulled on a stocking cap and gloves. She and Amelia followed suit. At the end of winter, thirty degrees was practically swimming weather, but this side of summer, it took a while for her blood to thicken.

Lee came around the front of his pickup, a blanket around his arm, and a steaming cup in each hand. He handed one to Elise. "Still like an oak milk latte?"

"Oh, bless your heart." She gratefully accepted her the coffee drink and sipped, letting it warm her insides and her heart. That he had remembered her favorite drink was endearing. Lee was still the gentleman, something she'd scorned in her early days as a feminist and physician. That was one of the many items she'd recorded on her "What I Did Wrong" list.

Amelia ran ahead, leaving her to walk with Lee, which was okay. Another change that had occurred over the past couple of months.

"Do you know what to expect?" Lee asked, his gaze straight ahead. "Did she give any hints of what we're supposed to do? Are we to read our sins aloud?"

Our sins. Boy, that was a truthful way to put it.

"I don't know. Our daughter is good at keeping secrets. You seem concerned."

He blew out a breath, and a frozen cloud drifted from

his mouth. "You could say I've had a revelation."

"You and me both." Elise stopped and turned to Lee. "How did two messed up people raise such an amazing daughter?"

"Probably that team we've enlisted. My players have been with me all along." He placed a hand on her back, and Elise let out a little gasp as he guided her forward. The slight touch was a surprise, but quite welcome, and felt very natural.

They reached a bench Amelia was wiping off. It looked over the lake that would soon freeze if today's weather kept up. Lee stopped Elise from sitting and spread the blanket over the cold cast iron. When sitting, they did not leave an Amelia-sized hole between them, but just enough to be discreet while allowing her to feel some warmth from his body.

Amelia stood in front of them, her arms crossed, and her hands rubbing up and down her arms. "I know from both of you that it's been a tough few weeks."

Lee grunted and Elise chuckled at his response.

"What you do with what you've learned is up to you, but I'm giving you one direction for today, and that's to listen. I read this quote from Steven Covey recently. 'Seek first to understand, then to be understood.' What that looks like will be different for both of you." She pulled her phone from her pocket. "I'm heading to Latte Fun to work on some schoolwork. You can meet me there."

Elise sipped at her coffee and stared out at the lake, waiting for Lee to speak, yet debating if she should set the tone for today.

"What do you want to do?" Lee finally said, pulling a crumpled piece of paper from his pocket. "Feel free to go first."

Was he being a gentleman or avoiding? Didn't matter, as she was glad to take the lead.

She turned to him, her knee barely grazing his, ignoring the desire to take his hand as well. "I won't rehash the affair. That's the easy *sin*, as you put it, to lay out."

Lee glanced down at his lap.

What to make of that, Elise wasn't sure, but she kept on. "I think what I've learned over the past three weeks is the that affair was the culmination of my other mistakes I made. Letting my career become my god and having an ego to match. Letting my gaze wander to greener pastures only to discover it was just dry grass painted green. That doctor had nothing on you except social status which, I've learned, really has no value at all. I put my career above you and Amelia. Yes, I was helping sick children, but was blind to the sickness creeping into our little family."

Lee raised a hand to his eyes. He was crying?

Still, she had more to say, the most important statement of all. She blinked back tears to get through it. "Basically, what it comes down to is that I messed up badly. I hurt you and Amelia and tossed away years together for my selfishness, and I can't tell you how sorry I am." Tears trailed over her cheeks. "I know I'm thirteen years late for this, but is there any way you can forgive me?"

She held her breath, waiting for a response, but Lee kept his head bowed. His hands were splayed open. His way of praying? Didn't really matter. Now was her time to sit quiet and listen, if not to Lee, then to God's whispers. She closed her eyes, folded her gloved hands around her coffee and listened to wind cutting through bare trees, to lake water fighting the freeze by lapping onto the shore, to cars motoring past on the highway behind them. To God's voice telling her that He delighted in her, that she was beloved, even with all her mistakes.

"I have a question for you." Lee's soft baritone slipped into her prayer.

She looked up. Nodded.

"That day here, when I proposed"—He made finger quotes—"did you anticipate, were you hoping for a real proposal?"

She reviewed that moment in her thoughts. It had been spring, and she'd just completed all her pre-med courses. Lee had treated her to a picnic not far from this very spot, then he got up on a knee and joy and dread shared equal places in her heart. No doubt she'd say yes, but was she ready to make that commitment, one her parents hadn't been able to keep?

Then he opened his hand. A key, not a ring, sat in his palm, and disappointment coursed through her. Elise didn't recall his exact words, but they did include an "I love you." They were also very practical. They'd save money by living together, especially since they often spent the night at his place. He was earning money as a journeyman electrician, and she was still accumulating debt. Then he'd promised to follow her wherever her job took her.

How could she say no to that? So they'd hugged, kissed, and then went back to his apartment for that night and every night thereafter. A real proposal never came, and she was okay with that.

Or so she'd thought.

"The answer's complicated," she finally said. "But in truth, yes, I'd hoped for a proposal, a ring, that special day where I got to be a princess and you were my prince. Silly, I know."

"No, it's not. I'm sorry I took that from you. I know we weren't believers then, but deep inside, I still knew something was wrong, like I was saying na-na-na-na-na-na to nature or something, even though that's what everyone did. Now I can see that was the beginning of our end."

He sniffled and wiped at his nose. "I did so much wrong, Elise." He shook his head. "I took you for granted. I think I knew you wanted to get married, but as long as you didn't complain, I didn't pursue it. I didn't listen to you. I made the decision for both of us without getting your input. When I inherited Grandpa's house and insisted we move in, I ignored your complaints that it was too far away from the hospital. I didn't hear your opinions about small-town life. And then I made the decision to be a stay-at-home dad without consulting you. With every misstep, I pushed you further away. Maybe you had the affair to get my attention—I forgive you a hundred times for that and for everything else—but by then it was too late. We were too broken and had no faith in God to restore us."

He sat up and wiped a hand over his eyes.

She longed to give him a hug, but kept her arms pressed to her sides. Her own mind swirled with his confession. For so long, she'd blamed solely herself, and honestly, her actions did the final and permanent severing, but Lee wasn't an innocent in this.

"It wasn't until these last months that I've considered my part in our breakup, that it's really my fault. When I pushed you away, what did I think would happen?"

"Oh, Lee." This time she did wrap her arms around him. Sobs wracked his body, and her tears wet his whiskered cheek.

"I'm sorry, Elise, for everything," he said into her shoulder. "I've confessed to God, to my team. That was easy. I know they'll forgive. But you and Amelia, that's the hard part because my selfishness tore us apart."

He pulled away, looked her square in the eye. His eyes still shone with moisture. "I know I don't deserve it, but can you forgive me?"

Elise took his hands, cupped them between her own, and resisted the urge to kiss away his hurt like she used to do. "I do forgive you."

He sighed and his shoulders lifted as if they no longer carried a heavy burden.

"But I have a question now." She kept his hands between hers, very uncertain of his answer, though she knew what she wanted him to say.

His gaze scanned hers and landed on her lips, then back up to her eyes. “I know what my feelings are telling me, but the last time I let them speak for me, I broke us. That can’t happen again.” He pulled his hands from hers then wrapped hers in his. “I think the important thing is to ask God what our next step is and really listen for His answer.”

Chapter Five

To say she was giddy was an understatement, even among this day-after-Thanksgiving crowd at the Mall of America. These past few weeks, Elise had almost felt like a schoolgirl in love for the first time.

She and Lee hadn't kissed. Nope. They hadn't even seen each other since the cold day at the Bemidji park, but they'd shared plenty of phone calls. No I-love-yous either. It was too early for that, but still she believed that was where they were heading.

Today was their final assignment from Amelia, though Amelia had already told them they'd passed the course and didn't really need this final step. Today was more about enjoying their time together.

With Christmas music playing over the loudspeakers, Elise squeezed among the shopping throngs, taking in the Christmas decor as she went. She loved it, but Lee probably couldn't wait to get home.

She passed Nordstrom on the way to their meeting

place, Macy's. In past assignments, nostalgia had played a role in the location chosen, but she and Lee had no past with Macy's, so she was curious.

Tantalizing scents of fresh-baked cookies and hot coffee drifted past, tempting her, but she'd wait until she was with the family.

The family. Huh. When was the last time she'd thought that phrase with a smile and hope? It gave her a little lift as she walked. She checked her watch and quickened her steps. She wouldn't be late, but being early never hurt, especially since Lee tended to be an early bird.

She took a right at the corner leading to Macy's and spotted Lee and Amelia on a bench. He waved her over and handed her a cup.

She sniffed at the opening. "Mint mocha?"

"Yep." Lee grinned. "You still like it, I hope."

"Oh, absolutely." She took a long sip and sighed. Just what she needed for a winter day pick-me-up. "And let me guess, yours is just a regular coffee."

"Real coffee, you mean, without all the junk ruining it."

"Dad." Amelia groaned. "You don't know what good coffee is." She held up her cup. "I got a gingerbread latte. It's divine."

"That's my girl." Elise nodded to her daughter.

"Well." Lee rubbed his hands together. "I know you two love the mall, and you can stay all day if you want, but the sooner I get out of here the better. What's our assignment today, Miss Aldrich?"

Amelia set down her coffee and took both their hands.

"Just this. Family."

Elise shared a glance with Lee, and his mouth lifted to the right, waking those butterflies in her stomach. His smile grew, which meant her expression gave away too much information.

"Lead the way." Lee gestured to Amelia then held out his hand for Elise. She looked at it for a second and another before grasping it, as if holding his hand was making a commitment.

Maybe it was.

Amelia led them to an escalator that took them to the first floor, then wound among shoppers until they reached an opening that led into the amusement park. "Remember when I was almost four and you guys took me here?"

Elise snapped her fingers. That was the connection. She'd forgotten all about that day-after-Thanksgiving event, probably because she'd wanted to put it out of her mind. She and Lee had argued that morning after a torturous Thanksgiving with her family, and they wanted to make it up to Amelia. Then they'd argued again after the trip. That day marked the beginning of their end. Thankfully, Amelia remembered the happy part of that day.

With Lee's hand in hers, Elise promised herself that she wouldn't make the same mistakes again. Today wasn't going to be another beginning of an end, but the prelude to a beginning.

Lee might despise shopping, but he was always game for amusement park rides. Well, maybe not fourteen years ago. Oh, he was a jerk that day, letting Elise know at every opportunity how much he didn't want to be there.

Thankfully, Amelia didn't remember the tension that had sizzled between him and Elise that day. He had no desire to go shopping, much less at the overcrowded megamall. Add that to the torturous Thanksgiving meal the day before—who serves tofu instead of turkey for Thanksgiving?—and that entire forty-eight hours ended with an argument that relegated him to the couch for a week.

Now, with Elise's hand locked in his, they waited in long lines, screamed on the coasters—well, Elise and Amelia did the screaming—and rested shoulder-to-shoulder on the Ferris wheel, all with contented smiles on their faces. This was how family should be.

"Ready for some food?" Lee asked after getting off a spinny ride.

Elise shook her head. "It'll probably all come back up. I used to be able to ride these, no problem."

"The joys of getting old."

"Watch it, buster." She elbowed Lee in his side. "You'll always be ten months older than I am, and I plan to age with grace."

"Babe, you're already succeeding."

Her cheeks blushed as red as a rose, which looked adorable on her. He squeezed her hand and whispered in her ear, "You're looking amazing."

Somehow her cheeks grew more red.

She squeezed his hand as they walked past the toy brick store. “Why don’t the two of you play for a bit. I need to find a restroom.”

“Sure thing.”

She tried to release her hand from his, but he held on to do something that had been on his mind since he saw her walking toward them this morning. It was a risk for sure, but he needed to know her feelings, so he kissed her on the cheek.

Her gaze rose to his, her mouth open in a O. Yeah, it had been worth the risk. He grinned as he released her hand.

Silently, she left for the restroom, and he watched the gentle sway of her hips as she gracefully cut through the crowds, until he could no longer see her.

Yeah, it was just a cheek kiss, but still, it was a signal to her that he cared, without promising a future. Yet. But he’d been praying, along with his team, for discernment, and he wasn’t getting any stop signs. Later, he might make a riskier move, but that depended on how the day went.

“You still love Mom, don’t you?” Amelia tore him back to the moment.

He shrugged and gestured to a table with loose bricks for people to build with. Did he love Elise? Boy, that was difficult to tell. Was it love or infatuation or him just wanting to have someone around when Amelia left for college? Or all of the above?

“I don’t know,” he said honestly as he stacked bricks

into a house shape. “I’m enjoying our time together, our talks. I’m enjoying not being angry with her. I feel lighter without carrying around a grudge. So, do I love her? Absolutely. But in love? We’ll have to see.”

“That’s all I need.” Amelia wrapped her arm around his back and leaned into him.

“So, does this mean your challenge was successful? That you’re staying home for Christmas?” He picked up the house he’d created and offered it to her.

She shrugged with a sly grin. “I don’t know. The day isn’t over yet.”

“So you’re saying when the clock strikes midnight, you’re staying home?”

“If you and Mom keep playing nice, there’s a good chance.” She set three brick people figures next to the house Lee had created.

That would be nice. Really nice, actually.

He glanced at his watch. “I think I can hold out another nine hours.”

“I think you can, too.”

They continued playing with the bricks, adding a Christmas tree outside, and a garage and truck.

“Are you two children having fun?” Elise knelt beside them.

“I am.” Lee thought about stealing another cheek kiss, but decided to wait until later when he might take a risk and go for her lips instead. Yeah, he’d do that.

Elise’s phone pinged, and her brows furrowed.

“Problem?” Lee gestured to a bench that another

couple just vacated. Amelia continued to build while Lee sat alongside Elise.

"I guess that depends upon your answer."

Uh-oh. Why didn't he like the sound of that? "What is it?"

"Mom and Dad are going to be at my brother's place for Christmas. Actually, the entire family plans to be there."

"Sounds like fun," he said sarcastically, then added with a grin, "Christmas with the crazy Kraemers."

"That's my family we're talking about."

"Hey, I'm just repeating what I've heard you say. I remember that Thanksgiving fourteen years ago. Besides, what does this have to do with me? I'm not stopping you from spending time with them." He certainly wasn't invited, and even if he was, he'd give a flat-out, "no way." They'd probably serve some kind of veggie ham.

"They want to see Amelia."

"Of course, they . . ." He cut his reply short then shook his head. "Christmas Day?"

"And Eve." She jutted out her chin, asserting her position.

"No." He shook his head. "I've had the trip to Wyoming planned since last Christmas. You had Amelia last year. You can see your family on your own."

"And we can't make an exception one time?"

He laughed. "If I was the one asking you to make an exception, can you imagine your response? You'd have laid into me for being selfish."

"Wow." She backed away from him. "You're right.

Instead, I'll lay into you now for being selfish. Mom and Dad are in their eighties."

"Barely."

"And who knows when we'll all have an opportunity to get together again. Amelia should see her cousins."

"I agree, which is why we're going to Wyoming."

Elise laughed. "And here I thought you'd grown up." She draped her purse over her shoulder and opened her mouth, but a shadow hovered over them, quieting both her and Lee.

Amelia stood above them, with her phone to her ear, her jaw tight and eyes glassy.

"Hi Katie." Her tone smiled, but the look she seared down on Lee and Elise was anything but friendly. "Yeah, I have good news. I'm coming to New York with you for my birthday and Christmas."

Lee's mouth fell open but he didn't dare say another word. His mouth had already done too much damage.

"Let's talk about this, Amelia." Elise patted the open spot beside her.

Amelia just held out her hand to Elise. "I'd like your keys. You two lovebirds can drive home together."

Chapter Six

The temperature inside the truck had been more frigid than the below-freezing temps outside. Elise could become the ice queen faster than any woman he knew, and she'd turned the cold shoulder on full blast for the past two hours on the drive home.

Not that he didn't deserve it. He was a selfish, unthinking, foam-at-the-mouth idiot. All of his apologies landed on deaf ears.

Elise's had as well.

So, she'd surrendered her car keys to Amelia, who'd torn from the mall faster than an Olympic skier racing downhill.

Now they had nothing left to say to each other.

How could a budding romance reconciliation wither in mere seconds? Worse than that, they'd included Amelia in their demise.

He sighed for what had to be the fiftieth time as he drove up the driveway of her house that was far too large for just two people, and Amelia was only there on weekends and every other holiday.

Elise clutched the door handle, turned to him. "I'm sorry."

His gaze barely brushed hers. "Yeah, me too."

"Why do we keep making a mess of things?"

"My only answer is that we're human, but I feel like that's just an excuse. I need to get home, get on the line with my team, pray it over, see if there's any way to salvage this mess."

"Same here." Elise opened the door, letting in a blast of cold air, then looked back. "For the record, I do care about you. My apologies up in Bemidji were real. I guess I was hoping to relive our past and forget about all the hurt in between then and now."

"Maybe we took it too fast."

"Maybe." She looked away then stepped out of the truck. "And maybe *we* never should have been."

With that, she closed the door, lightly, but it felt like a slam to his heart. He put the truck in gear, backed down the driveway, and tore home.

Then he gathered his team on a conference call and prayed for wisdom to pull out a win.

"Hi Debbie, I have a problem," Elise said over the phone.

When she'd arrived home, Elise had taken a hot, soaking bath to relieve her muscles, but that did nothing to ease the burden of her heart. So she got on the phone, first to Luella, then Gloria. They'd both prayed over her following her confession, but Debbie always seemed to have insight the others didn't.

"I gathered you did." How did Debbie always know what Elise was feeling or thinking? Even over the phone? "Amelia's here, by the way. Asked if she could stay the night. I told her it was up to you, at least for a couple more weeks."

When she would turn eighteen. Elise felt far too young to be a mother to an adult, but that was the reality, and that scared Elise to death. She didn't want Amelia to make the same bad choices, to go through the same hurt, yet she knew that this side of heaven, that wasn't a possibility.

"Yes, she has permission."

"You want to talk about it?"

"No." Always was the response to Debbie's question. "But I will." She inhaled a slow breath and let it out to the count of ten. "We went to the megamall for Amelia's last assignment, we were having a great day, and then I threw a monkey wrench into our perfect day." She explained the argument from her perspective and then told about Amelia's angry departure. "Was that just a teenager whim, did she overreact, or did we really blow it?"

"A question for you?" That was always Debbie's response, it seemed. "Did you or Lee let Amelia have any say in your Christmas plans?"

Elise closed her eyes, relived the argument, hoping for something that would show she and Lee hadn't both been selfish, but no. They'd fought over her as if she were a doll, not their precious daughter.

Finally, Elise responded. "No. We didn't."

"Hmm." Dead air meant Debbie was thinking, and Elise had learned to give her that space.

But an idea formed in the silence. "What if . . ."

Elise relayed her idea to Debbie, who affirmed it might work. Then she scheduled tomorrow afternoon on the family app for her, Lee, and Amelia, and called Lee to explain.

And they even prayed together.

Whatever happened tomorrow was in God's hands.

Chapter Seven

Lee sat alongside Elise in their booth at the supper club where they'd begun Amelia's assignment over three months ago. This time, the room was lit with Christmas lights on each window, and a large, undecorated pine filled an entire corner of the room. "Do you think she'll show?"

"I think so." Elise toyed with her napkin. "But she is a teenager."

"True." He took a sip of his coffee and wished he had something to munch on to bide the time. The easy banter he and Elise had shared just a day ago had hardened into silence. They'd apologized and forgiven each other, but had nothing else but remorse to share between them.

"There she is." Elise sat up straighter, as did Lee.

Amelia slid into the booth opposite them. "Well, this is interesting." Her poker face gave away nothing.

"We have an in-class assignment for you." Elise slid a fresh notebook across the table. On the top she'd written, *Home for Christmas Challenge, part 2.*

That got Elise to smile, anyway.

"Go ahead." Lee made a turn-the-page motion with his hand.

And she did. She stared at the page for a second then glanced from Elise to Lee. "Talk?"

"Yep," Lee said. "We learned that we've done all the talking and didn't give you an opportunity to voice your opinion."

Her eyes lit up. "Oh."

"And we'll sit here and listen." Elise folded her hands on the table. "And be honest. There will be no judgment from us."

"Are you sure?" She looked from Lee to Elise and back again.

"Hundred percent," Lee said. "I put on my big boy pants this morning, so I can take it."

That made both Amelia and Elise chuckle. A little levity didn't hurt, right?

"Okay, then." Amelia folded her hands over the notebook and bowed her head.

Silence was not what Lee expected or wanted, but he then realized Elise's head was bowed as well. Duh. He followed suit and lifted this afternoon up to God. He prayed that God would give Amelia the right words and that they would do a work in his and Elise's hearts. He prayed that whatever the outcome of today's class would be God's will and nothing else.

"Yesterday was my goal." Amelia began.

Lee gripped Elise's hand, and thankfully, she didn't

pull away.

"I have this vague memory of being at Camp Snoopy." Amelia's eyes lit up. "And riding the train and carousel and the two of you smiling together. We were a team. A family. Maybe that time sticks out because I saw so little of it growing up."

Wow. What a sad depiction of his parenting.

"And whenever I'd go to Katie's house, I saw an intact family. They weren't perfect—Katie'll tell you that—but even in their imperfections they stick together. Same goes for her uncles' families in Brainerd and New York. I thought going to New York with Katie, I'd get to experience the family Christmas I've missed out on, not the celebrate-at-Dad's-on-Christmas-Eve and then shuttle-to-Mom's-for-Christmas-day experience."

Elise's hand gripped his harder.

"I just wanted one Christmas." Amelia shrugged. "Just one Christmas at home. With the three of us. Even if it was pretend. And then I saw the way you two were getting along, and I hoped for something I hadn't planned. To think that maybe the two of you would get together again, was really beyond my hopes."

She sighed. "And then yesterday was so much fun, until it wasn't. I wanted you to see me as a grown-up, not your little girl who you had to use an app to make sure you each got equal time with me, because none of it was fair."

Lee felt sick to his stomach at how he'd treated their daughter.

"When you decided for me yesterday, I felt I didn't have

any other choice. If you'd invited me into the discussion, I'd have told you that I wanted one Christmas at home, just the three of us. Not the Kraemers and not the ranch, but just one Christmas at home where we'd go to the candlelight service on Christmas Eve. We'd all stay the night, and then I'd wake up and hurry to the fireplace to see what Santa brought and then have you both there for breakfast before opening presents. A real family. Together. I know you've always told me that just because I want something, doesn't mean I'll get it, but I hoped. And I prayed so hard."

Amelia sniffled and Elise handed her a tissue.

No surprise, Elise was wiping her own eyes.

"You're right. About everything." Lee clenched his jaw so his emotions wouldn't spill out.

"Is it too late for this year?" Elise gripped Lee's hand so tight, he felt he'd lose circulation.

"So no Kraemers and no ranch? You can get along for two days?"

"We won't be perfect," Elise said.

"I don't expect perfection. Just one Christmas together. Just the three of us, and whatever happens from there, happens."

Lee exchanged a look with Elise, and she nodded. "Then that's exactly what we'll give you."

Epilogue

1 Year Later

Amelia's alarm went off at six a.m. Way too early on a normal day for a college student, but this was Christmas Day, the celebration of Jesus's birth. And she was home, in her own bedroom, with Mom and Dad sleeping under the same roof, if not in the same bed.

For the second year in a row!

Last Christmas had been a bit awkward with her parents not quite knowing how to function under the same roof. She'd seen their glances, trying to figure out where they stood with each other, but they'd survived without one argument.

And this past year, they'd even grown to like each other again. That had been more than she dared hope for.

Amelia hurried downstairs and found her stocking hanging from the fireplace mantel right in between Mom's and Dad's. She flicked a switch, turning on the fireplace.

Something soft nudged her ankle, and she bent down to pick up Data, the tabby cat Dad had adopted after she went off to college. He'd always told her he wasn't a cat person, but the truth lay in Data's purr. This kitty did love attention.

"You're up." Dad, wearing his pj's, came out of his office, where he'd spent the night on a blow-up mattress. He'd refused to let Mom lie on the floor, and Mom hadn't argued.

"Of course." Keeping Data in one arm, she hugged her dad with the other. "Any sound from Mom's room?"

"Other than her snoring?" He chuckled, thinking he was hilarious, but the truth was Mom did snore, though she'd deny it.

"You're so funny." She set down the cat and knelt by the Christmas tree to see what she'd find with her name on it. Seeing gifts for Lee and for Elise under the tree, something that hadn't happened for years until last year's challenge, made her do a kneeling dance.

She loved seeing that her parents still liked each other. Beyond that, she didn't know. Two days home with only Dad around, and then the candlelight service last night, didn't give her any clues. If romance didn't blossom between them, that was okay, too. As long as they could have family Christmases.

Behind her, a door opened and closed, then another door closed.

"Mom's up," Dad said. "Want some breakfast? Coffee?"

"I'll pour myself a coffee, but can we do the stockings

before breakfast?"

"Before, huh." Dad looked to the bathroom. Smiled. Nodded. "Yeah. That would work."

Okay, that was strange. But whatever. Dads were naturally strange, right?

About twenty minutes and two cups of coffee later, Mom finally came out of the bathroom, looking awesome. That was a clue, for sure. Back at her house, Mom didn't care what she looked like around Amelia, but here? Very interesting, indeed.

Dad handed Mom a cup of coffee. "Sorry, it's just black."

"That's perfect." She squinted at Amelia. "Someone insisted on getting up at six a.m. on my day off."

"Can you blame me? It's Christmas!"

As Mom and Dad sat side by side on the couch—another clue?—Amelia leaped from the floor and hurried to the fireplace. She removed all the stockings and handed them out. Yes, she was acting like a five-year-old, but she had years to make up for.

"You go first," Dad said as Data jumped up on his lap.

"Yay!" Amelia sat cross-legged on the floor and dug into her stocking. A toothbrush. A pair of socks with *Star Wars* characters on them. A pair of panties. "Dad!"

He held up a hand and pointed to Mom. "I had nothing to do with that, believe me."

"I hope not." Amelia dug in again and hit pay dirt. Chocolate. She poured the rest of the stocking onto the floor and grabbed a Hershey's Kiss. "Breakfast."

"I don't think so." Mom held up her stocking. "Me next?"

"Nope." Dad pulled it away. "You got to go first last year. My turn."

Mom pretend pouted. "Fine. Go ahead."

Dad also got a toothbrush, a pair of socks, and chocolate. Instead of underwear, he got new winter driving gloves. "Would you look at that?" He tugged them on and winked at Mom—another clue. "Santa knew just what I needed."

"I wonder how." Mom smiled at him, and her toe nudged his.

Okay, they were no longer giving clues, but this was affirmation. Amelia could barely rein in her excitement.

"What's in yours?" Dad sat up taller and leaned over, trying to sneak a peek into Mom's stocking, but she pulled it close to her chest. "Patience, dear."

Dear? Amelia did a small jig where she sat.

Mom reached into her stocking and pulled out a toothbrush, socks, and chocolate, then dug back in. Something was stuck in the toe.

By the grin on Dad's face, Amelia knew it was something special.

Mom finally pulled out the item.

A ring box! Amelia squealed.

"Lee, you didn't." But the shine in her eyes told Amelia that she certainly hoped Dad did.

Dad winked and put a finger to his mouth as he got on one knee on the floor.

Mom's fingers shook as she lifted the lid, then she leveled the meanest stare Amelia had ever seen, at Dad. "I am not going to just live with you."

"What?" His eyes twinkling, he took the ring box from Mom and showed it to Amelia.

A key. No wonder Mom was livid.

Amelia took her dad's place on the couch, snuggled against her mom.

But then Dad, still kneeling, reached into his pajama pocket, kept whatever he dug out tight in his fist, so Mom couldn't see it, but let's face it, they both knew what he held.

He took Mom's hand. "You know I'm not one for speeches, so I'll make this short. This past year has been the best one of my life. It's amazing what happens when you let God take control of your life, thanks to our daughter, who is the most mature young woman I've ever met and who will be the best special ed teacher out there."

"I agree." Mom kissed Amelia's cheek.

"Thirty-some years ago when we moved in together, I was clueless about the amazing woman who'd agreed to share my life, but now, only due to the grace of God, she's back in my life in a fuller and more beautiful way than ever before."

He opened his hand, and Mom gasped.

Amelia did too.

The ring was understated, really. Three strands of rose gold woven like ivy.

"It's perfect," Mom said under her breath.

It really was.

"Would you be willing to give me another chance, Elise? Do it right this time." His voice shook, and he closed his eyes, but not before a tear fell. "Will you marry me?"

"Yes! Yes!" Amelia jumped up and clapped and then realized she hadn't listened to Mom's reply and slumped back on the couch. "Sorry. Go ahead, Mom. Give Dad your answer."

"Well, if you weren't screaming loud enough for the neighborhood to hear, you would have heard me say, absolutely yes."

And Mom and Dad kissed. Really kissed. Not that peck on the cheek she'd seen him give her, but a full, not very child-friendly kiss either, but that was okay. Amelia was an adult now, so she could watch them and be ecstatic for them without telling them to get a room, which would be a really bad idea.

And to think, this never would have happened if she hadn't challenged them to be home for Christmas. Well, that and a whole bunch of prayer.

If God could reconcile these two, which was about as easy as moving mountains, then He absolutely could do anything.

Put on then, as God's chosen ones, holy and beloved, compassionate hearts, kindness, humility, meekness, and patience, bearing with one another and, if one has a complaint against another, forgiving each other; as the Lord has forgiven you, so you also must forgive. And above all these put on love, which binds everything together in perfect harmony.

Colossians 3:12-14

Author Note

It's been over two years since I've sat to write a story, two years since I've typed the end as my husband's Alzheimer's has changed priorities in our lives. Still, God nudged me. Scratch that, He shoved me face first into telling this story of reconciliation that I didn't know needed writing.

I first met Lee, Amelia, and Elise in *Pieces of Granite*. They were side characters in another broken family story and insisted they be allowed to reconcile. Who was I to argue?

I loved the role that grown-up Amelia played in her parents' lives. I also recognize that their story is a unique one and not all marriages or relationships can be or should be reconciled, but this story gives hope for those that can. And that hope can only come from a God who forgives and moves mountains.

A God who was born miraculously over 2000 years ago to become the Savior of this world.

Praying you have a blessed Christmas!

Acknowledgements

This story came together in one week, which is very quick for me, but it could not have been written without the prayers of my Mosaic sisters. My sister Gayle read my unedited draft and offered enthusiasm for the story and much needed encouragement. And Lesley An McDaniel managed to squeeze proofreading this story into her busy schedule to tighten make this story pretty.

Books by BRENDA S. ANDERSON

THE MOSAIC COLLECTION
Broken Together
Pieces of Granite
A Beautiful Mess
A Beautifully Broken Christmas

THE MOSAIC COLLECTION ANTHOLOGIES
Hope is Born: A Mosaic Christmas Anthology
Before Summer's End
A Star Will Rise: A Mosaic Christmas Anthology II
The Heart of Christmas: A Mosaic Christmas Anthology III
All Things New
A Thrill in the Air
Sounds Like a Plan

COMING HOME SERIES
Pieces of Granite (Prequel)
Chain of Mercy
Memory Box Secrets
Hungry for Home
A Christmas Homecoming – A Novelette in *A Star Will Rise*
Coming Home – A Novelette in *All Things New*
The Home for Christmas Challenge – A Novelette in *A Thrill in the Air*

THE POTTER'S HOUSE BOOKS | ONE
Coming Home Series Novellas
Long Way Home
Place Called Home
Home Another Way

WHERE THE HEART IS SERIES
Risking Love
Capturing Beauty
Planting Hope

THE POTTER'S HOUSE BOOKS | TWO
Where the Heart Is Series Novellas
Hands of Grace
Song of Mercy
Season of Hope

https://brendaandersonbooks.com/books/

Books in The Mosaic Collection

MID-YEAR ANTHOLOGIES

Before Summer's End: Stories to Touch the Soul
Song of Grace: Stories to Amaze the Soul
All Things New: Stories to Refresh the Soul
Dancing in the Rain: Stories to Shelter the Soul
Sounds Like a Plan: Stories of Change and the God Who Doesn't
BirdSong: Stories of Promise and Hope

CHRISTMAS and WINTER ANTHOLOGIES

Hope is Born
A Star Will Rise
The Heart of Christmas
A Whisper of Peace
A Thrill in the Air
A Weary World Rejoices
Skipping Winter

JOHNNIE ALEXANDER

The Mischief Thief (Rose & Thorne #1)
When Memory Whispers (Echoes of War #2)
Journey of the Heart (Unseen Valor #1)
Beneath a Rare Blue Moon (Unseen Valor #2)

BRENDA S. ANDERSON
A Beautiful Mess
Pieces of Granite (Coming Home Prequel)
Broken Together (written with Sarah S. Anderson)
Chain of Mercy (Coming Home #1)

ELEANOR BERTIN
Lifelines (The Ties that Bind #1)
Unbound (The Ties that Bind #2)
Tethered (The Ties that Bind #3)
Flame of Mercy (Burning Bright #1)
Flicker of Trust (Burning Bright #2)

SARA DAVISON
Lost Down Deep (The Rose Tattoo Trilogy #1)
Written in Ink (The Rose Tattoo Trilogy #2)
Every Star in the Sky (two sparrows for a penny #1)
Every Flower of the Field (two sparrows for a penny #2)
Every Bird That Falls (two sparrows for a penny #3)
The Color of Sky and Stone (In the Shadows #1)
This Little Nowhere, Nothing Town (The Rose Tattoo Trilogy short story collection)

JANICE L. DICK
The Road to Happenstance (Happenstance Chronicles #1)
Crazy About Maisie (Happenstance Chronicles #2)
Calm Before the Storm (The Storm Series #1)
Eye of the Storm (The Storm Series #2)
Out of the Storm (The Storm Series #3)

DEB ELKINK
The Red Journal
The Third Grace
Vagabond Come Home

CHAUTONA HAVIG
Spines & Leaves (Bookstrings introduction)
Hart of Noel (Bookstrings "Noella")
Twice Sold Tales (Bookstrings #1)
Clock Tower Bound (Bookstrings #2)

MILLA HOLT
Into the Flood (Seasons of Faith #1)
Through the Blaze (Seasons of Faith #2)
Within the Storm (Seasons of Faith #3)
Amid the Ashes (Seasons of Faith #4)
After the Frost (Seasons of Faith #5)
Home Town Melody (Rhapsody of Grace #1)
Small Town Harmony (Rhapsody of Grace #2)
Old Town Symphony (Rhapsody of Grace #3)

ANGELA D. MEYER
This Side of Yesterday
Where Hope Starts (Applewood Hill #1)
Where Healing Starts (Applewood Hill #2)
Where Joy Starts (Applewood Hill #3)

STACY MONSON
When Mountains Sing (My Father's House #1)
When Valley's Mourn
Open Circle
Shattered Image

LORNA SEILSTAD
More Than Enough
Watercolors

CANDACE WEST

Through the Lettered Veil (Windy Hollow #1)
Among the Kindled Embers (Windy Hollow #2)

OTHER

Totally Booked: A Book Lover's Companion

About the Author

Brenda S. Anderson writes authentic and gritty life-affirming fiction that shows God at work in people's messy lives. She is a founding member of the award-winning, nontraditional publishing company, The Mosaic Collection. When not writing, she enjoys live sports and theater, walking along the shores of Lake Superior, and sharing hot cocoa with friends and family. She lives near Minneapolis with her newly retired husband and their twin mischievous kitties, Mauer and Morneau.

Connect with Brenda

BrendaAndersonBooks.com

Facebook | Instagram | Goodreads | BookBub

MosaicCollectionBooks.com

BRENDA S ANDERSON

Life-Affirming Fiction

BrendaAndersonBooks.com

www.ingramcontent.com/pod-product-compliance
Lightning Source LLC
Chambersburg PA
CBHW060656190726
48289CB00002B/441

* 9 7 8 1 9 5 1 6 6 4 1 2 1 *